STILL
AS
DEATH

Books by J. A. Kazimer

Lucky Whiskey Mysteries

A Shot of Murder
Still as Death

The Assassins Series

The Assassins' First Date
The Assassin's Heart
The Assassin's Kiss

The Deadly Ever After Series

The Fairyland Murders
The Lady in Pink

The F**ked-Up Fairy Tale Series

Curses!
Froggy Style

The Wilde Crimes Series

Dope. Sick. Love.
Shank

Stand-Alone Books

Cuffed: A Detective Goldie Locks Mystery
Haunted in Hollywood: The Adventures of Loey Lane
Holy Socks & Dirty Demons: A Hellish Paranormal Romance

STILL
AS
DEATH

A Lucky Whiskey Mystery

J. A. KAZIMER

BEYOND THE PAGE
PUBLISHING

Still as Death
J. A. Kazimer
Beyond the Page Books
are published by
Beyond the Page Publishing
www.beyondthepagepub.com

Copyright © 2020 by J. A. Kazimer
Cover design by Dar Albert, Wicked Smart Designs

ISBN: 978-1-950461-75-2

For my "best" friend, Kaley August (Kazimer)

I'd tell the world how awesome, smart, beautiful
and brave you are, but you'd hate that, so let me just say,
YOU SUCK AT CARDS.

Chapter 1

The sign announcing Jack's seventy-fifth birthday threatened to crash down as I struggled to pin it up with a dull tack. The chair I stood on wobbled with my every move, making me regret the decision to use it as a ladder. Not that I had much of a choice. After all, the Gett Bar didn't have an actual ladder. And why would it? Drunks and ladders didn't mix much, like whiskey and tequila.

I had less than an hour to finish decorating for the party. A party that had to be perfect. After all, seventy-five was a big milestone. One my grandfather had almost missed due to a heart attack that had nearly killed him nine months ago.

A heart attack that changed both of our lives.

Since the day I returned home to take over Jack's care as well as Lucky Whiskey, nothing had seemed the same.

I surely wasn't.

My life, which had once consisted of late-night Hollywood parties, now entailed waking at four a.m. to check cask strength or churn the delicate mash. Not to mention the hours I spent looking for a head distiller willing to work in the Florida Everglades. If I was honest, it wasn't so much the Everglades that bothered the most eager of candidates, but rather the murder of our last distiller.

That and the Getts.

The Gett family and my own, the Luckys, had a long history of sabotaging each other. Not unsurprising since we both ran whiskey distilleries in a town the size of a shot glass.

The chair swayed once more and I stifled a string of curse words. Before I fell, a pair of strong hands gripped my waist. I gasped when I realized exactly who those hands belonged to— "Grodie" Brodie Gett. Unfortunately, the nickname I'd given him in grade school had never quite stuck, much to my dismay. Unlike the one he'd thrust on me.

"What are you doing, Charms? You'll kill yourself," he drawled in that good ole boy manner, even though he'd spent the last ten years living all over the world as an Army Ranger. But he was home now. Like me. The town was in our blood, much like the whiskey business. I'd fought it for as long as I could, but every day whiskey became more and more a part of me.

1

Where I once dreamed of accepting an Oscar, I now fantasized about the perfect blend.

A sad testament to my love life.

"Don't call me that," I growled. "My name is Charlotte. I know nine letters are tough to remember for you, but do try." I slapped at his hand. Thankfully he didn't remove it, for neither the chair nor I were stable.

"Don't go getting all huffy, Charms. I'm saving your life. Again."

"Again? You're kidding, right?" I glared at him. "If anything, you nearly got me killed."

He winced, humor leaving his face. "Let me say again how sorry I am—"

"Unless you're apologizing for lying, for *years*, about the water tower, I don't want to hear it."

One of his dark eyebrows hitched upward. "Water tower? What about it?"

I bit my lip to keep from screaming. Three months ago, when he thought I was dying, Brodie confessed to, years ago, painting the town's water tower to read *Getting Lucky*. Which was bad enough. But he'd also put the blame on me.

Now he acted as if I'd imagined the whole sordid confession.

I wasn't close to forgiving him yet. Though I had to concede he'd made a fairly good crime-solving partner. I wondered how he was at hanging party decorations.

"All joking aside, what the hell are you doing? You're going to fall and crack that stubborn head of yours."

"What does it look like I'd doing? Balloon animal tricks?" I snapped.

He grinned. "As much as I'd like to see that, I'm afraid you're gonna break your neck instead. Jack surely will be surprised then." His hand shifted when I rocked back a step. "Come down, and I'll pin the sign up."

"Fine." I gave an affected huff, blowing a wayward piece of tawny hair from my eyes. My once stylish A-line hairdo had grown out, leaving me a shaggy mess. Here in Gett, the only two hairstylists were Mrs. Bennet, an old, nearly blind woman with a flair for bowl cuts, and Nadine Rogers, who loved teased hair, the higher the better, and gossip. Having lived with bowl cuts for the first seventeen years of life as well as more than my share of cruel gossip, I opted for trimming my own split ends. "I have plenty of other things to do before tonight anyway," I added.

Without a warning, he swept my knees out from under me, forcing me to grab his neck or risk immediate injury. He held me against him, swinging my legs back and forth. I couldn't help but laugh, which made him act up even more. Just like when he'd pull my pigtails in grade school.

"Let her go before we have a problem," a voice growled from behind us.

Brodie swung to face the intruder. My eyes shot wide when I caught sight of the man dressed in gator-hide boots, with matching belt, designer blue jeans, and a light sapphire-colored shirt that cost more than I made over the last year.

"Marcus?" I muttered, shocked. I hadn't talked to my ex-boyfriend, Marcus Savage, since leaving Hollywood. In truth, I hadn't thought much about him either. "How . . . what are you doing here?"

"You know this . . . guy?" Brodie asked, his voice hard, almost as much as his muscles pressed against me. I looked to him, and then to Marcus, who wouldn't stand a chance if Brodie truly lost his temper. Marcus wasn't puny by any stretch of the imagination, but his muscles were the gym-sculpted kind — an illusion, like most things in Hollywood. Brodie, on the other hand, likely knew fifty ways to kill a man with a whiskey bottle.

I poked Brodie until he let me down. He kept his hand on my waist though, as if irritating Marcus on purpose. I pinched his arm. Hard. He winced but didn't release me. "Marcus, this is . . ." *My friend* didn't sound quite right to explain my relationship to Brodie, not with years of baggage between our families and us, so I decided on, "Brodie Gett. Brodie, Marcus Savage."

Brodie's face looked blank, like he didn't recognize Marcus's name. Even though Marcus spent years playing a hero on the TV show *War Dogs*. Not too surprising since Brodie spent little time in front of the TV, unless it was to watch hockey or football.

"Good to meet you." Brodie held out his hand.

Marcus didn't take it. Instead, he reached for my arms, pulling me toward him for an embrace. Thankfully Brodie had let go of my waist. Last thing I needed was to be involved in a testosterone-fueled tug-of-war. I fell into Marcus. He bent to kiss my lips, but I moved my head in time. His lips hit my cheek, leaving sixty dollars' worth of La Mer lip balm imprinted on my skin.

I stepped back. "What are you doing here?"

"I came to see my girl and celebrate your grandfather's birthday. I can't wait to meet him." He smiled, the amber flecks in his eyes sparkling. "And see the town you talked so much about."

My forehead wrinkled. I didn't remember ever discussing Gett, Florida, nor Jack with him. Especially since my feelings for the man who raised me after my parents' deaths, along with the town, were complicated at best.

"But . . . we . . . ah," I mumbled to the man I'd thought was my ex. I didn't want to hurt his feelings, not after he came all this way, and especially not in front of Brodie, who was watching our exchange with a hard grin on his lips. "How did you find me?" I said instead, glancing around the back room of the Gett Bar, the only place large enough to fit half the town for Jack's party tonight—people who expected a bash bigger and better than Rue Gett's eightieth birthday blowout last year. A lot was riding on tonight. Not only was I honoring my grandad and his legacy with the unveiling of this season's small batch, but the future of Lucky Whiskey might very well hang in the balance. If I couldn't manage to secure a loan from the Gett Savings & Loan to buy a new still, we were sunk.

Marcus shrugged. "I asked at the Gett Diner. About seven people pointed this way. God, I would die in a town like this without any privacy."

I wanted to laugh. Gett had nothing on Hollywood when it came to gossip. By my second date with Marcus, my face, along with commentary on my bra size, hairstyle, and weight had been splashed across at least two tabloids. One of which claimed a shocking pregnancy.

He wasn't finished. "This place doesn't have a four-star hotel or even a three-star one. Instead I'm registered at this awful place the next town over. How do you stand it here?"

"Perhaps it would be best if you move on, quickly, before something even worse happens," Brodie snapped.

I flinched, never before having heard that tone from the normally good-humored Gett. What was going on with him? My eyes caught his, but no emotions were revealed in his rigid gaze.

Marcus's shoulders drew back, chest puffing forward.

The tension in the air was denser than a glass of Gett Whiskey. Enough was enough. With an eye roll, I stepped between the two men. I had much too much to do to waste my time dealing with this ridiculousness. "Listen, Marcus," I began.

"I missed you so much," he said, reaching for my arms again.

I ducked away. "That's . . . nice. But I'm really busy right now setting up for Jack's party. Maybe we can talk later."

"Oh," he said, his eyes darkening. "Of course. I'll see you at the party then."

Before I could dissuade him of the idea he moved toward the door. A couple stopped him for a photo. Leaning between them, he smiled into their camera phone. Once it clicked, he patted the man on his back and gave the woman a hug. "Make sure to tag me in it," he said.

Brodie snorted, shaking his head.

I could only imagine what Jack would think when he met Marcus. My grandfather didn't like anyone I dated, let alone someone he considered a Hollywood type. *Type* was always said in a snarky slur. "I don't need this right now," I whispered.

"I couldn't agree more," Brodie growled. "Now hand me that damn tack."

I did as he ordered, unable to meet the judgment surely in his eyes.

Chapter 2

I checked my watch for the fourth time in the last ten minutes. It was a little past five now. I still had to shower off the bar grime before my meeting with Rue Gett's manservant and closest friend, Marshall. He had graciously agreed to cater the party with all of Jack's favorites — BBQ ribs, fried catfish, mounds of potato salad and plenty of whiskey to wash it all down. All my hard work over the last month putting together Jack's party was about to pay off. My grandad would surely be surprised. And secretly pleased, though he would grumble loud enough for all to hear.

"Can you add a few more seats there?" I asked Brodie. He nodded, grabbing a stack of folding chairs by the door. For the last hour, Brodie had worked his way around the bar, setting up tables and arranging chairs on my orders. A rarity, for in all my days he'd yet to listen to my orders. No matter how many times I tried to force him to during our brief stint as investigators a few months ago.

"Was that Marcus Savage you were chatting with?" asked the copper-haired woman behind the bar. Willow Jones stood a few inches taller than my own five-six, leaving me staring at her chin. I sighed. This wasn't the first time someone had asked me that question since Marcus had left the bar. I felt like wearing a sign around my neck saying *Yes, I know Marcus Savage*. By now our encounter, repeated word for word, was all over Gett.

"Are you two dating?" she asked when I didn't say anything.

Unfortunately the answer to that question wouldn't fit on a sign.

Brodie stepped forward, a smile on his lips. "Charms wouldn't date that guy. She's much too into me."

Willow and I shared a snort.

He laughed, grabbing his chest and staggering back a step. "Ouch. After all I've done, hanging signs and moving furniture? That hurts. Really. I'm wounded."

"Seriously, are you dating him? I loved him in *War Dogs*." Willow's face fell. "Broke my heart when they killed him off last season."

"Not nearly as much as it did his," I said with a grin. "Marcus brooded for a full month."

6

"So you are dating. I knew it," she said. "If I had a celebrity boyfriend I'd tell anyone who'd listen. Why didn't you tell us he was coming to see you?"

I bit the edge of my nail, peeling off the fresh coat of pearl pink nail polish I'd applied yesterday. One more thing I now had to do before the party. I dropped my hand. "I'm as surprised as anyone to see him."

"Maybe not everyone," Willow said as she swiped her rag across the bar. "Marcus left with Evan."

"What?" How could that be? My cousin, Evan, and Marcus barely knew each other. They'd met for half a day when Evan came out to LA to visit a few months before I'd left town. The visit ended with Evan borrowing a thousand dollars from me, which he'd yet to pay back, and an assurance he'd call before showing up on my doorstep again. Suffice it to say, we were far from kissing cousins.

Brodie patted my arm, his hand warm, skin rough. "At least he didn't rent some stupidly expensive sports car. That getup is going to be enough for the town to laugh at tonight."

I smacked his hand away. "I'm glad you find this so amusing."

"Not as much as you'd think." His gaze drifted to the dirt parking lot beyond the doorway. "Rue won't like anyone but her upstaging Jack tonight."

I winced at the mention of Brodie's grandmother, the formidable Rue Gett. She was a woman to be reckoned with. She was the matriarch of the Gett clan and the main instigator in a variety of Lucky family woes over the years. She and Jack had been at each other for as long as I could remember. Jack claimed that their rivalry kept them young. I suspected it would be the death of me though. "We wouldn't want that." Brodie raised an eyebrow, and Willow stifled a laugh. Too late I recognized how sarcastic I sounded. "What I meant to say . . ."

"I got it," he said with a chuckle.

My face heated.

"Now, where do you want that ridiculous blow-up gorilla?"

Chapter 3

"Girl, why're you making me wear my churchgoing clothes?" Jack asked a few hours later as we stood in front of a full-length mirror in the hallway of the Lucky family monstrosity. The house had eight bedrooms, though only two of them were ever used. Faded yellowing wallpaper hung throughout, left over from my grandmother Jennie, who'd departed this world nearly thirty years ago. We'd never met yet we shared similar features and the same tawny hair. Jack swore we also shared a stubborn streak, but I suspected mine came directly from his DNA.

I tugged at the sleeve of his white cotton dress shirt. It hung way too loose on his frame. He'd lost so much weight. To be expected, the doctors insisted. A man whose sole diet had consisted of fried foods was bound to lose a few pounds once he began eating right.

"Are you listening to me, Char?" He snapped his gnarled fingers in front of my face. "Tell me what's going on right this instant. You're not involved in another murder, are you?"

I held back a snort. Jack had been far more *involved* in the murder case than I had. Sheriff Danny Gett had arrested him for the murder within days of my finding a corpse in a Lucky Whiskey cask. "No dead bodies to report," I said. "I just want you to look nice for your dinner with Billy and Sweet Jayme." Sweet Jayme and Billy had agreed to take Jack to the party after their dinner without him being any the wiser.

He exhaled long and loud like he had when I lied as a teen. Not that I lied to him all that often. "I don't know what you're up to, but I don't like it."

I leaned over his shoulder to kiss his cheek. His gray whiskers tickled my lips. "I love you. Now, remember to take your pills before you go." I waved to the kitchen, where a glass of water sat on the oak table along with three butterscotch-colored prescription bottles.

"One for these days, girl . . ." he muttered as he turned around and headed for the kitchen, leaning on his cane for support. I took the opportunity to run upstairs and shower. The blast of icy water felt wonderful on my heated skin. How could it be eighty degrees with eighty percent humidity in the middle of winter? What was wrong with this place?

After washing my body with my favorite gardenia-scented soap, soap I could only get at a boutique in LA, I dried off and quickly dressed in one of my few nice dresses. This one was all black with a deep V along my spine, showing off plenty of skin. I tugged at the hem, frowning slightly. I wanted to look good but worried showing off this much thigh just might give Jack another heart attack.

Beyond my window, the beam of a flashlight caught my eye. Someone was walking around outside, too close to the distillery for my peace of mind. The last thing I needed was another murder victim to be found in our rackhouse.

I stormed down the stairs and out of the house, adrenaline rocketing through my body. Rocks dug into my feet, reminding me that I lacked both shoes and common sense. Rushing out of the house, in the dark, to confront an intruder wasn't the smartest move.

I should, at the very least, go back to the house to grab the shotgun Jack kept under his bed. Before I made up my mind to do just that, I recognized the man attached to the flashlight. Relief washed over me, as well as more than a little annoyance. "Marcus? What are you doing out here?"

His head shot my way and he flicked off the flashlight. A handsome smile curved over his lips. "Charlotte, I'm so happy to see you. I wasn't sure if you were inside your distillery or in the house. I guessed wrong." His gaze lingered on my body, eyes heating with appreciation. "You look beautiful."

My normal state of self-consciousness disappeared. Maybe the dress did look good. Maybe my hair wasn't quite such a mess. Maybe I wouldn't screw everything up tonight, thereby further damaging the Lucky name. I hated my insecurity. A sad effect of living in Gett. I'd laid naked on an autopsy table for my appearance on *NCIS*, and didn't blink. And yet here I felt very much like an awkward teenager with pimples most of the time.

I blew a lock of hair out of my eyes, trying not to wince when I noticed the gator-skin boots on Marcus's feet. I'd recently developed a healthy respect for the large leathery beasts and didn't like seeing one wrapped around Marcus's feet.

"Will you show me around?" he asked, nodding to the Lucky family home. Peeling paint, once white, now looked yellowed with age and neglect. Though the distillery shone with a fresh coat of paint. Luckys had our priorities in order.

Jack was still inside the house, so instead I motioned to the distillery next to us and the rackhouse building beyond. "Let me show you around the distillery instead. It was built over a century ago." I didn't add that it smelled like it too.

Why ruin the surprise?

Chapter 4

I inhaled sharply as we entered the building that housed Lucky Whiskey. The scent of fermentation mixed with aged timber tickled my senses, comforting in a way no one outside Jack would understand. It was the scent of home. Of family.

Marcus didn't agree. He started gagging as we passed the malting room, where germination of the grains happened. Admittedly, the yeasty perfume was known to knock even hardened distillers off their feet. "Sorry," I said, motioning to the water and barley shoots just beginning to form. The tiny green buds promised a very smooth blend. "It's an acquired scent."

"No problem," he said with a laugh, once he managed to keep his lunch down. His head tilted to one side, letting a lock of hair fall across his eye. The overall effect of vulnerability didn't pull at my heartstrings as much as it once had. "The distillery is smaller than I expected." A frown pulled at his lips. "How much whiskey can you make?"

Small? I glanced around the four thousand square feet of space that didn't even include the rackhouse, which doubled the area in vertical space alone. Then again, Marcus spent much of his time in a fourteen-thousand-feet soundstage. The distillery probably did look undersized in his eyes. I tried not to take offense. "We cask about fifty thousand gallons a year." Unexpected pride rose in my voice. "That doesn't include the small batches."

"Impressive." Before I could warn him, he tapped the industrial-sized copper still closest to us, a still that hovered around two hundred degrees. Yelping, he yanked his hand away, and then blew on the red mark on his palm.

I grabbed his injured hand in mine, assessing the damage. It didn't look too bad. No blisters in sight. "I'm sorry. I should have warned you. Those are very hot."

He pulled his hand away, giving me a boyish smile. We stood inches apart, close enough my heartbeat sped up a beat. A lone finger caressed my chin. "Can I ask you a questions, Charlotte?"

I nodded slowly.

"Have you considered selling this place and coming back to Hollywood?"

Those were far from the words I'd expected to hear. I stepped back, stumbling a bit on the pitted flooring. "I couldn't . . . This is Jack's baby. As long as . . ." My throat ached at the thought of losing my grandad.

"I didn't mean to upset you," he said, pulling me to him. "I just miss you. Miss us. We were good together. We can be again. If you'll only trust me. I can take care of you, of everything . . ." He motioned to the distillery.

I pushed against him, freeing myself from the embrace, more than a little annoyed by his assumption that I wanted or needed anyone to take care of me, let alone the distillery. I took a calming breath before speaking, "Marcus, it's not that I don't appreciate you coming all this way — "

"Charms? You out here?" Brodie's voice rang through the open doors.

I jumped, as if caught with my lips on Jack's prized whiskey stash. "Over here."

Brodie's tall frame appeared, dressed in his finest, which equated to a pair of Levi's sans holes. His eyes flickered over Marcus and then fell on me, a hint of question in their cobalt depths.

"I was just showing Marcus around the distillery." I quickly explained why he'd found Marcus and I alone, in the darkened distillery, though I had no idea why. Brodie and I weren't even friends, let alone anything more. Not that I was interested in more. Arrogant men, who believed they knew best, weren't my type.

"Oh," Brodie said, his lips arching downward. The frown shifted to a snarky smile when his eyes landed on Marcus's gator-skin boots. I knew just what he was thinking and I didn't like it.

Before I could say so, Brodie inclined his head to Marcus. "Savage, let me know if you want to see a real distillery."

The offer, while seemingly politely given, was a reference to his wrongheaded belief that the Getts made better whiskey — an argument we'd had a hundred times since I'd started running the distillery. "As in real disgusting," I said without pause.

One dark eyebrow rose as he focused his icy blue gaze on me, slowly giving my dress a once-over. None of the male appreciation Marcus had shown me appeared in Brodie's eyes. "Shouldn't you finish getting ready for the big party?"

I gave Marcus a smile, and then glared at Brodie. "I'll be back in a minute."

Brodie's mocking laughter followed me out the door.

Once back upstairs, irritation, nothing more, had me adding another coat of rusty-colored lip gloss to my lips as I checked my dress in the mirror. What did I care what Brodie thought? Even as the words flickered through my brain, I gave my hair another tousle. Catching the telling action, I stuck my tongue out at my reflection and then headed back downstairs.

Before I reached the front door, Marcus's raised voice drifted through the window. I winced, thankful for Jack's slight hearing loss. Marcus gestured around wildly, though I couldn't quite understand his words. The small, brittle smile on Brodie's face indicated his anger. Not a good sign.

I slipped out the front door, rushing to where Marcus and Brodie stood on a dirt path lined with ruts as long and deep as the Lucky family history. The trail led from the back of the house to the distillery. I knew each rut, each indentation. Like the Lucky family history, the grooves were deep and abiding.

"What is going on?" I said once I reached them.

Neither man answered.

I slammed my foot down to gain their attention, accidently striking the toe of Marcus's boot. His eyes flew to mine. "We were just getting clear on a few things. Weren't we, Gett?"

"If you say so."

"Clear on what?" I asked.

"You," Brodie bit out the single word.

My hands went to my hips. "What about me?" When neither answered, I prompted in a tone edged with steel, "Marcus?"

"I was just assuring Gett that his escort services are no longer required for tonight," he said as if he had any right to make such a decision. Or really any decision about my life.

My temper flared, heating my already warm skin.

"Good," Brodie said. "I have better things to do with my time."

The anger I felt at Marcus changed direction. I never asked for Brodie's help. He was the one who insisted on accompanying me tonight. Before I said as much, he added, "Rue asked me to come by to tell you Jonas Moore will be at your party tonight."

13

The hurt at his earlier statement vanished at the name. I clapped my hands together as my mind swirled with possibilities.

"Who's this Moore guy?" Marcus asked, sounding jealous. Which was ridiculous. What I had in mind for Jonas Moore had nothing to do with sex. For one thing, he was married to the most beautiful woman in Gett. Secondly, he was old enough to be my father. And finally, what I wanted from him would last longer than any old romance.

I debated how much to say in front of Brodie. The less he knew about Lucky Whiskey business the better. When Marcus asked again, Brodie answered for me. "Manager of the Gett Savings & Loan. Looks like you have some competition for Charms's affections."

I glared at him.

The rat had the nerve to shrug, his eyes burning. Like he had any right to be mad at me.

"Oh, sweetheart," Marcus said, opening his arms wide, "if you need a loan . . ."

I shook my head. Money from Marcus was the last thing I needed. "It's nothing like that." Though it really was. Our main still was on the fritz, and much too soon it would break for good, and we'd be left up whiskey creek, losing over half of our production. I'd been in talks with Jonas and the bank for weeks regarding a two-hundred-and-seventy-thousand-dollar loan. Funny how a year ago I drooled over a pair of Jimmy Choo's, and now my dreams were of a twenty-five-hundred-gallon copper still.

Moore's attendance tonight could signal that we'd secured the loan. Once that happened, I could finally breathe again. I needed to think, to form a plan of attack for tonight—something Brodie excelled at, but before I could ask for his thoughts, he said, "See you around, Charms." He turned on his heel and disappeared around the house. The roar of his Jeep followed, as did the crunch of gravel as he shot down the driveway.

"Shall we go?" Marcus asked, offering me his arm.

I hesitated for a moment before finally taking it.

Chapter 5

As I walked into the Gett Bar, Marcus's warm hand in mine, I stopped, letting my gaze slide around the room. The place looked amazing. Far more so than how I'd left it a few hours ago. Silver steaming serving trays lined the bar with townsfolk adding plates of home-cooked dishes next to them, one after another until there was enough food to feed everyone in Harker too. The smells of savory treats swirled around the room, mixing and mingling much like the guests.

Nearby sat a wooden cask with the Lucky name branded in thick black scorch marks on the side. Glasses were stacked three feet high around it. Balloons in a variety of colors floated in the air, adding to the festive atmosphere. Best of all, the big birthday banner Brodie had helped me secure announced for all to see that this was a very special day indeed. Townsfolk had come out in mass to bring this party together. And I felt a gratitude I'd never felt before to the people of Gett.

I thanked each person, gripping their hands tightly, though most were far more interested in taking pictures with the famous Marcus Savage. Even the one man of God in Gett, Pastor Matt Reeves, waited his turn for a chance to take a selfie with a celebrity.

Much to my delight Marcus graciously agreed to each photograph, smiling for shot after shot. And even taking a few of his own. Usually with his arm slung around me. While it was nice to feel appreciated, I had work to do before Jack arrived. Slipping out from under his arm, I moved off to check the temperature of the cask, making sure the whiskey was a perfect sixty degrees.

The room quickly filled as eight o'clock drew near. Our bookkeeper, Crystal Green, with her new boyfriend, Willis, arrived looking a bit disheveled but happy. Adam and Derrick Best walked in right after, thick, wavy dark hair slicked back for the occasion. The twin brothers had a history of ruckus behavior, but two better bottlers couldn't be found. They worked for Lucky, like their father and uncles before them. Proud of each bottle bearing our name. Next came Jonas Moore and his wife. I couldn't remember her name. Though I could've asked any of the gossips, for her marriage to Jonas had tongues wagging for the last six months.

Before I could make my way across the room to the couple, an elderly woman, her features too sharp to be called beautiful, approached. Brodie stood next to her, looking annoyed. "Sorry we're late, Charms. Some ass—Excuse me, some person slashed two of the tires on my vehicle."

"Don't look at me," I said with a quick grin. "I love that Jeep."

"Funny," he snorted.

The woman, not one to be ignored, tapped my shin with her cane. "Isn't that dress a little short?"

"Rue," I said with a tight smile. "So nice to see you. Thank you for coming."

She held up a silver flask of what I assumed was Gett Whiskey. "I brought this along just in case."

"Now, Rue," Brodie said to his grandmother, a hard smile firmly affixed to his face. "Give Charms's whiskey a chance. What's the worst thing that can happen?"

Rue laughed, which, honestly, sounded like a cackle to my ears. "The Luckys are finally the death of me?"

I rolled my eyes. "You'll outlive us all. Now, if you'll excuse me . . ."

Before I managed to make my escape, Jack's thin frame appeared in the doorway. He looked stunned by the crowd of people, his mouth hanging wide. "What's . . . all this?"

In all my years, I'd never seen him more at a loss for words. I smiled, rushing forward. "Happy birthday!"

A grin split his features, almost obscured by a growth of whiskers. "Did you pull this together, girl?"

I nodded. "With plenty of help."

He grabbed my shoulders, pulling me to him. His lips touched my cheek and I inhaled the scent of oak and whiskey, of yeast and sour mash—his scent. It clung to him like the Lucky name. "Thank you."

Tears filled my eyes. I quickly blinked the wetness away, for Jack hated tears. "You are welcome. Now come in and enjoy the first sip of the small batch." I didn't have to ask him twice. He bounded to the bar like a much younger man, with a strong heart. The healing power of whiskey pride.

I followed behind him, serving him a glass of my first small batch. In that moment I understood his passion, his struggle, and what he'd lost nine months ago. Whiskey was more than Jack's way of life; it was his life. His passion. His one true love. A part of me understood his obsession, the way in which the perfect drop rolled around your tongue, inducing memories of fields of peat and heather, even in the hellish heat of the Everglades.

Jack took the glass, his hands shaking slightly. He held it up to the light, swirling the whiskey in the glass. The amber color refracted into a rainbow that danced along the bar.

I swallowed as he raised the glass.

The liquid slid forward along the glass to his lips.

Sweat beaded on my palms.

He drank deeply, his face blank. Seconds ticked by.

Had I screwed up and served the cask before its time?

He lowered the glass, giving nothing away.

Why had I pushed the small batch's release? What had I been thinking?

Finally, Jack looked into my eyes. "Good finish."

My heart soared. For Jack, *good finish* equated to a rousing cheer. In whiskey, finish beat everything, including flavor. He didn't say anything more. He didn't need to. With a wave of his hand, he ushered the crowd forward to taste the small batch.

An hour later, the party was in full swing. People danced, ate, and drank, all with gusto. I talked with what seemed like everyone in town over the age of eighteen. My throat grew raw. I waved to Nancy Jeanne, who was breastfeeding her newborn baby at the back of the room. The child looked like every other member of the Gett clan—too damn cute for their own good.

Music swelled in the air, an array of oldies and current hits. Marcus asked me to dance when a Luke Bryan song burst from the speakers. I took his offered hand in mine. He maneuvered me closer, the scent of leather and vanilla of his Tom Ford cologne tickling my senses. His strong arms felt good around me, and for a moment I entertained the possibility of a long-distance relationship.

It would feel good to have someone on my side for a change. For the past nine months, I fought an uphill battle to gain the respect of those around me. The glares of the townspeople whenever they glanced up at the water tower hurt more than I'd admit. Add in Jack's constant badgering about the distillery, and Brodie being Brodie, and having Marcus around didn't seem so bad.

The idea didn't stay long.

Marcus wasn't the man for me, and I really wasn't the woman for him. Our lives were too different, our worlds even more so. Besides, I had more important matters to consider than romance at the moment. Lucky Whiskey for one. Without a new still, we were looking down a dark, deep hole I wasn't sure I could dig us free from.

My gaze scanned the crowd, searching for the one man who could help—Jonas Moore.

Jonas sat at a table toward the back of the room with his younger bride, a plate of rib bones in front of him. His fingers were coated with the rich red sauce, which he wiped on a napkin as he rose to greet me following my dance with Marcus. "So good of you to invite us, Charlotte. I hope Jack's enjoying himself."

I waved to the center of the room, where Jack held court, a group of his oldest friends surrounding him, all sipping Lucky's small batch. Even Rue. "So far, so good."

Jonas glanced down at the woman seated next to him. "Charlotte, have you met my wife, Grace?"

I smiled at her, aware of how dumpy I must look in comparison. She wore her hair up in the latest fashion, streaks of gold shimmering in the dim light. The makeup on her skin, what there was of it, looked just as flawless. "I don't think we've had the official pleasure yet."

She stuck out her hand. "It's nice to meet you."

"Are you from around here?" I asked, unable to place the slight twang of her accent. Was it mid-Atlantic? As an actress I appreciated the way in which words formed on people's lips. It was a subtle indication of a wealth of buried characteristics and personalities.

She shook her head. "No, Tampa. Jonas and I met about six months ago while he was there looking for some investments."

Jonas laughed. "We were married a week later. Best investment I ever made."

18

She smiled up at him with something akin to hero worship in her eyes. "It was love at first sight."

For a brief moment, I wondered how falling in love instantly would feel. Honestly, it sounded pretty awful. "It's very nice to meet you. Please enjoy the party." I turned my attention to Jonas. "I'd love to finish our discussion about the loan for a new still, if you have time on Monday?"

His eyes widened as if shocked that a woman might care more about financials than social mores. Thankfully he recovered quickly and agreed to meet. A weight lifted from my shoulders. Everything would be all right. We'd get the loan, and Lucky Whiskey would survive, and even thrive.

Walking back to the center of the party, my happiness dimmed a bit at the sight of Brodie Gett dancing with Mindy Drift. The blond beauty queen twirled until he caught her in his arms, her laughter ringing over the steady beat of the music. The two of them made a striking pair. Damn him.

I turned toward the bar for a drink. "Lovely party," Pastor Matt Reeves said with a warm smile as I approached. I couldn't help but smile back. The pastor was young, no more than a year or two older than me. He had sandy blond hair and a boyish grin that put one instantly at ease. He'd only recently moved to Gett, after spending a year on a mission in India. I leaned in, trying to catch his next words over the music and free-flowing whiskey. "Jack is lucky to have you in his life." A faint flush rose on his cheeks. "No pun intended."

I held back a snort. I was the lucky one. Jack had taken me in at the darkest time in his life, after he'd lost the son he'd loved, the heir he'd shaped to take over the family business. What had a man in his fifties known about raising a five-year-old girl? Though he'd agreed without hesitation. Family, to him, meant everything.

"Are you enjoying yourself?" I asked, motioning to the string of single ladies waiting to ask him to dance. All the mothers of Gett worked tirelessly to catch him in their daughters' clutches, as they'd long given up on both Danny and Brodie Gett. Not a hint of gossip was attached to the pastor's squeaky clean name. Surely odd in a town this size, but something I could appreciate. I longed for the day not a word was whispered about me.

The pastor's next words brought me back to the conversation at hand. "If only they paid me this much attention during Sunday service," he grumbled.

I couldn't help but laugh at his tone. Marcus, who stood a few feet away, picked his head up, focusing on me. He left the local spinster Tessa Franklin and joined me. I introduced the two men while anxious mothers circled. Marcus preened at the attention. I didn't have the heart to tell him the interest wasn't all his.

A few minutes later, Marcus excused himself. A good thing too since Sweet Jayme waved at me from the kitchen. I checked my watch and nodded back at her. It was time for the cake. She had outdone herself in that regard. Three days baking and decorating had resulted in a chocolate lover's dream. The cake was large enough to feed the entire town and shaped like a barrel of whiskey with the words *Jack Lucky* across the front.

Carefully, and with Billy James's help, she wheeled it toward Jack, who sat at a table in the center of the room. Jack drained the whiskey in his glass as the cake approached, his eyes focused on the sheer number of lit candles.

I moved closer. Jack didn't look happy, his eyes flat and hard. I couldn't understand why until I overheard Marcus say the word *blessing* to him.

My stomach lurched.

No, no, no.

Before I could shout the words to stop the impending madness, Marcus grabbed my hand, jerking me in front of the cake. He lowered himself to his knee.

All eyes flew our way.

The music skidded to a halt.

I searched for a way to escape. My heart slammed in my chest, and my body grew hotter than all seventy-five candles on Jack's cake. I tried to breathe but couldn't take in any air to my lungs.

Across the room, my eyes caught Brodie's, pleading for his help.

He turned his back and walked away.

The panic increased until my head swam.

The crowd pressed in around us, blocking everything from my view but Marcus and the aqua-colored Tiffany's jewelry box in his hand.

How had this gone so wrong?

Now, rather than a success party and launch of the Lucky small batch, the only thing people would remember was my panic-induced heart attack.

I tried to extract my hand from Marcus's without causing more of a scene, but he held tight. Almost too tightly. My skin reddened under the pressure. Once again I tried to pull back from the man on the floor in front of me, but to no avail.

"Charlotte, when you left Hollywood, I thought I would survive without you. But after all these months apart, I now know the truth," he said in a booming voice used on soundstages and large theaters.

"Marcus, I—"

"I know, sweetheart. But let me get this out and then you can say yes." His grip grew harder on my hand. I tried not to flinch. "Charlotte Lucky, will you make me the luckiest—" He paused for a chuckle, "man, and—" Jonas Moore, pale and soaked in sweat, stumbled forward, clutching his chest. He made it as far as Jack's whiskey barrel–shaped cake before falling face-first right into the frosted creaminess.

Cake flew in all directions as Jonas crashed to the floor, dead.

Chapter 6

Sheriff Danny Gett rushed forward as Jonas hit the floor. He quickly started CPR while a call went out for Lester, one of the county's few paramedics. Brodie held Grace Moore in his arms. Danny checked Jonas for a pulse one more time and shook his head.

Pastor Matt stepped forward, motioning to the deceased man on the bar floor. "May I, Sheriff?"

Danny nodded, allowing the pastor to kneel next to Jonas. Grace cried softly. I didn't know Jonas well, but Grace's grief pierced my heart. Even now, I remembered how I felt watching the twin oak caskets of my parents, both draped in flowers, being lowered into the wet ground.

Pastor Matt brushed his hand over Jonas's unfocused gaze, lowering the dead man's eyelids, as he said a prayer for the dead, mouthing words he'd likely said a hundred times before. Words that offered little solace to those who loved Jonas.

Once Lester and his ambulance arrived, he quickly place Jonas's body on a gurney and zipped it inside a black body bag. I swallowed hard at the finality of the sound.

My eyes fell on Jack. He looked far too pale for my peace of mind. "Are you all right?" I asked, my voice rough, as if I'd drank a bottle of Gett. After all, it was less than a year since Jack suffered a heart attack that had nearly ended his life. Jonas hadn't been so lucky.

"Forget about me, girl," he said. "I'm sorry your big moment got ruined."

I frowned. "Big moment?" Other than launching the small batch, which was a success, tonight had been about Jack.

"Getting engaged. Did you forget already?"

"Oh, Jack," I began. "I'm not —"

Brodie loomed behind me, casting a shadow over us. "I'm taking Grace home," he said. "Can you wait with Rue until I get back, or will your *fiancé* be upset?"

Why did everyone assume I'd said yes to Marcus? I glanced down at my ring finger, shocked to see a platinum band with a large diamond solitaire set on top of it. When did that happen?

I blamed my not having noticed the fact I'd gotten accidently engaged on the shock of watching Jonas die. I'd never actually witnessed death before. Not up front and in person. It wasn't like in the movies. Peace wasn't found on Jonas's face. In fact, he'd looked horrified and in pain, his mouth nearly as wide his eyes.

Instead of answering Brodie, I moved toward Grace. She sat in a chair by the door, her arms around her body as if seeking comfort. She no longer looked young or carefree. Her eyes were red-rimmed, cheeks scarlet from tears. But that was the only color on her face. She was so pale, her hands so cold when I took them in my own, I worried for her. I rubbed her hand. "I'm so sorry for your loss."

She nodded numbly, eyes unfocused.

"Can I do anything for you?"

She blinked and then her gaze focused on me. "How could this have happened? He said he wasn't feeling well yesterday but seemed fine today. Oh, God, what am I going to do?"

Guilt curled in my gut, which was ridiculous. Eating ribs and drinking whiskey hadn't killed him. At least doing those things tonight hadn't. Over a lifetime sure, but not because of my invite, I reminded myself.

"Grace," Brodie said as he came over to where we sat. "I'll drive you home."

She slowly nodded.

"Maybe you shouldn't be alone tonight," I said. "I can . . ."

"It's all right," she said firmly. "I called my brother. He's driving in from Naples and will be here soon."

"Please call if you need anything," I said, passing her a napkin with my cell number on it.

She took it, her eyes flooding with tears again. "Thank you."

Brodie helped her to her feet, and slowly they made their way out of the bar. Grace glanced over her shoulder, her eyes glued to the spot where her husband had expired. Brodie urged her forward.

"Are you ready to go?" Marcus said to me a moment later. "This sticky frosting is not good for my skin." He rubbed at a spot on his shirt where a bit of cake had struck when it showered us following Jonas's face-first fall into it.

23

My own skin felt just as sticky, and I longed for a hot shower, but I couldn't leave. Not yet. And not with Marcus. Not tonight. While we desperately needed to talk, tomorrow would be soon enough. I glanced down at the ring on my finger.

First thing in the morning.

Chapter 7

The next day, before I could drink my first sip of the heated chicory slug Jack called coffee, my phone nearly exploded from a sudden rush of notifications. I groaned, a bad feeling settling in my chest. With dread I checked my iPhone. The bad feeling slipped into full panic as I read each alert. Some were texts from my Hollywood friends, most of whom I hadn't heard from in nine months. The messages were all similar, all asking for dirt on my recent engagement to a man who could aid their careers. The other notifications came from my social media accounts.

But the worst, by far, was the glossy shot on the front page of *TMZ* featuring Marcus on his knee in front of me. As usual, he looked wonderful while I looked shell-shocked and a bit like a woman raised by wolves in the wild.

I read and reread the misleading article, annoyed that they not only misspelled my name but barely mentioned what happened directly after. My accidental engagement had upstaged a man's death. Every time people thought of Lucky Whiskey, they'd think of death. Or the woman who broke the heart of a television hero. And I would break his heart, or at least our accidental engagement. It was top on my to-do list.

I glanced at the time stamp on the article, which was barely two hours after Jonas's death. How had they gotten the pictures so soon?

This was bad.

Plenty of men in the whiskey business already took issue with a female distiller, let alone one who was splashed across the covers of the tabloids.

I needed to rectify the situation as soon as possible.

• • •

An hour later, I stood outside the Harker Motel, which offered clean rooms rented by the week. Paint peeled from the stucco walls, muting the once bright yellow color. A small balcony peeked out from the room where Marcus was staying. The rails around it had rusted to near black. I suspected one small push and it would give way, crashing to the pavement below.

Running my hand down my jean skirt, I took a deep breath, preparing the "it's not you" speech in my head. Which was true. This wasn't so much about him as it was about me. I didn't want the same things as I did nine months ago.

Though I had no clue what it was I did want now.

I prayed Marcus would understand.

Slowly I climbed the concrete steps to the second floor. Marcus's room was two from the end, in an alcove that overlooked a small side parking lot. This section of rooms offered a bit more privacy than the others, if you kept the blinds firmly closed and the lights off. Marcus had gone the opposite route, and instead his door stood wide open. A TV blared from a room nearby.

I approached Marcus's room, each step feeling as if my rhinestone-coated sandals had lead weights attached. For a moment I stood there, gathering my courage.

"Charlotte?" Marcus said from behind me. I jumped in surprise, grabbing the rusted railing to steady myself. I feared it might break away so I quickly released it. Marcus reached out to steady me, his strong grip tight on my arm, as if he didn't care to let go.

Once my heartbeat returned to normal I looked him up and down. His hair was wet, curling slightly at the end, like he'd just taken a shower. He wore a pair of sweats and no shirt. His tanned muscles rippled as he led me into the motel room, though the sweat beading his forehead ruined the overall effect. Florida definitely wasn't for him, as it had barely reached seventy degrees outside.

The air inside the room was heavy and smelled faintly of cigarette smoke and new carpet. A poorly painted landscape with irregularly shaped mountains and purplish shrubbery hung over the bed. I recognized the artist, Wendell Dicky, the owner of the motel.

Everyone in Gett had, at one time or another, been gifted with a similar art piece. Jack's hung in the back of a closet, buried under fifteen years' worth of junk. I appreciated Wendell's courage to put his work in the world, if not the art itself.

The rest of the motel room appeared clean and well-tended with the small exception of the frayed edges of the bedding and the creak of the mattress as I sat down on the edge. Marcus sat next to me. The mattress sunk further under his weight until I feared it might swallow us whole. I righted myself, my eyes meeting his. "Marcus, we need to talk."

A frown settled on his handsome features. "I'm not sure I like your tone."

What could I say? He was bound to dislike my words far more. "It was very nice of you to come all this way . . ."

He smiled, reaching for my hand. The one with the damn ring still attached. "I'd walk a million miles for the touch of your lips."

The vaguest of memory flickered in my brain. Had I heard those words on his lips before?

Before I could ask, he leaned in, kissing me. His lips were so persistent, pressuring me to open for him. For a moment, I allowed and even longed for his warm touch. But soon enough I regained my senses, jerking away. "We can't."

His blond eyebrow rose in a carefully crafted way, an expression he'd used often in *War Dogs*. The fact he now used it on me killed whatever qualms I carried about breaking the kiss. I pulled at the ring on my finger, but it refused to budge. "Listen, Marcus, while I appreciate your visit and all this . . ." I tugged harder at the dammed ring. "I can't marry you."

His face twisted as his eyes darkened. "But *I'm Marcus Savage*."

Considering he screamed each word at top volume, I suspected everyone in the motel, as well as the entire city block, knew exactly who he was. "Calm down." I stood, backing away from the rage tightening his body. "I should've told you yesterday, before . . ."

He leapt up, grabbing my shoulders. His fingers dug into my skin. Red marks, sure to become bruises, formed under the pressure of his hands. I tried to pull away but he held firm. "This is all because of that Gett," he said darkly. His fingers flexed harder. I yelped, yet he didn't seem to care. "I saw how he was looking at you. And you at him."

"Marcus, let me go. Now." I shoved at him as hard as I could. The motion propelled me backward, and thankfully out of his grip. I banged into the nightstand, knocking over a heavy brass lamp. It missed my sandal by an inch. I reached down to pick it up, holding it in front of me as if to ward off an attack.

The action seemed to draw Marcus from his rage. His features softened, growing pleading as he whined, "I told Evan this wouldn't work."

My blood pressure rose at the mention of my cousin. "What does my cousin have to do with any of this?" Evan and I were barely on speaking terms. He wanted to sell the distillery, to cash in on Jack's legacy. I refused to even consider it.

"What?" He shook his head. "Nothing, of course. I love you, Charlotte. Can't live without you."

The words, while they sounded right for a man who proposed just last night, didn't ring true. The tone was off, like love was an afterthought. "You'll be fine," I said, rubbing the sting from my shoulders. "Millions of women would be happy to marry you."

"But I need you." His face reddened, causing the vein by his temple to stand at attention. "You have to marry me!"

"I most certainly do not," I said in a hard voice.

His thick wide hands reached for me again. I leapt away, dropping the lamp as I ran from the room as fast as my legs could carry me. For the first time since high school, I thanked Mr. Bergan, the Harker High track coach, for bullying me into wind sprints.

Marcus dived for me, missed, slamming face-first into the doorframe. I took the opportunity to dart down the stairs, taking two at a time. "You'll be sorry for this," he yelled at my retreating form loud enough for the entire motel to hear. "I'll make sure of it."

His words echoed in my ears as I jumped into Jack's pickup, locking the door behind me. I sat in the driver's seat, my breath coming in painful gasps. Marcus didn't move from the balcony, though his eyes burned me in place. If looks could kill, I'd be as dead as Jonas Moore.

Chapter 8

I drove back to the nearly empty distillery, my hands shaking. It wasn't until I started adding yeast to the wooden washback tanks that I noticed Marcus's engagement ring still on my finger. I once again tried to yank it off, but it still refused to give. No matter how hard I pulled, the band won't let go, just like Marcus.

After I finished with the tanks, I checked the cask strength of a few waiting barrels with the long tube used to suck up whiskey from a cask known as a thief. A brand-new one I'd purchased shortly after accidently stabbing Roger's body with my old one three months before.

Not many people outside the business understood the importance of whiskey proof. A few degrees either way and the cask would turn into moonshine, illegal to possess or sell in Florida.

I didn't need jail time added to my already lacking resume.

I tested each cask, happy when they came in around seventy percent. Next I grabbed a hard oak paddle carved by my father over thirty years ago and worked in the malting room, stirring the grains in preparation of germination. Hot yoga, in terms of sweat produced, had nothing on stirring the malt. After a few hours, my arms ached and my stomach grumbled, reminding me I hadn't eaten since last night.

I wiped the sweat from my hands and headed out of the distillery to the house. The sun had long gone down and I was full-on hangry. I dove into the refrigerator for some leftovers. I tore into a half rack of ribs, enjoying every barbequed slathered bite. I washed it down with a Diet Coke, letting the icy coldness dance over my tongue.

Once I wasn't in danger of killing anyone who crossed my path due to hunger, I relaxed on the couch, flipping through an old issue of *People* magazine. Celebrities, the beautiful people, stared back from each page. A full spread of the current *War Dogs* cast, minus Marcus, caught my eye. I flipped to the next page and read an article on the latest Marvel movie to hit a box office record.

Surprisingly no pangs of longing for Hollywood filled me. Life here in Gett was easier in many ways. Of course, I'd also seen two dead bodies in three months. A record, I was sure. Except for undertakers. Not once had I seen a corpse, at least one who remained dead after the director yelled "Cut," in the glittery lights of LA.

A knock sounded at the door. I reluctantly rose to answer it, the muscles in my legs quivering slightly at the disturbance. I peeked through the peephole. Last thing I wanted was another run-in with Marcus. The vaguest of an outline appeared in the doorway. I flipped on the porch light and the figure came into focus.

Brodie Gett, looking hard and lean, leaned causally against the wooden railing of the porch, one leg kicked over the other. I wasn't fooled. Knowing Brodie, he was coiled and ready to spring at the least provocation. The good ole boy façade didn't fool me any longer. He held up a hand in a sheepish wave when I opened the door.

"Is everything all right?" I asked, my heart pounding harder. Since receiving the original call about Jack's heart attack nine months ago, and then his subsequent arrest only three months prior, paranoia filled me every time the phone or doorbell rang. It felt like I was always waiting for the next shoe to drop, or a murderous maniac to ring my bell. The almost constant state of anxiety was taking its toll, yet I didn't know how to stop it.

Moore's death and the incident with Marcus certainly weren't helping.

Brodie gave me a half smile that failed to reach his eyes. In the dim light of the porch, his left eye looked red-rimmed and bloodshot. Was he drunk? Though he spent an inordinate amount of time at the Gett Bar, I'd yet to see him soused.

"Can I ask you something, Charms?" he asked, giving me his back.

"Of course." I stepped onto the porch, wrapping my hands over my arms to ward off the chilly night air. His head bobbed in acknowledgment but he didn't speak for a long moment. "Brodie," I said. "What's going on?"

He slowly turned to me, his face covered by the deep shadows unaffected by the dim lighting. "I was at the Gett tonight."

Like every other night, I wanted to say, but something held my words back. Brodie didn't look to be in a teasing mood. In fact, he

30

looked downright uncomfortable, shifting from one foot to the other. "Okay," I said slowly.

"Are you really going to marry that guy?"

"What?"

"Savage. Are you going to marry him?"

"Not that it's any of your business," I began. "But the answer is no. I don't have any intention of marrying him now, or ever."

Silence built between us until he finally said, "Good."

I frowned. "What does it matter to you?"

"It doesn't."

The stab of pain in my chest surprised me. Did I want it to matter to Brodie? Did I want him to care? I nearly laughed at the ridiculous thought. Grodie Brodie and I would never reach that level of friendship, let alone any other sort of relationship. Our blood promised as much. "So why are you here?"

"I just . . . Where did you get those?" He jerked his large hand toward my shoulders.

"My tank top?" I asked, confused. Brodie wanted fashion advice at nine a night? It wasn't like he cared about his own wardrobe, so why was he interested in mine?

"No. Those." Each word was colder than the previous.

I glanced down, unsure of what he meant. Then I saw the dark purple bruises on my shoulders, bruising shaped like the fingers of a hand. I ran my own fingers across the marks, surprised to find them tender to the touch.

"Did *he* do that?" Without waiting for me to answer, he stormed off the porch and to his Jeep parked in the driveway. Gravel crunched under his boots with each determined step.

"Brodie, wait," I yelled, my pulse pounding in my throat.

He stopped but didn't turn.

"Don't do anything stupid." Through the lump in my throat, I added, "Promise me."

Rather than answer, he leapt into the driver's seat and tore down the drive. I watched until his brake lights disappeared. Only then did I return to the house, my stomach in knots.

Chapter 9

I spent the rest of the night in a state of constant anxiety and anger, at Brodie, at Marcus, and at myself. I could fight my own battles. I didn't need Brodie going off half-cocked on my behalf. What gave him the right to think I needed him? My fingers curled around the magazine in my hands, crumpling the paper.

"Damn it, Char girl," Jack said, slamming down his untouched glass of amber liquid. "A man can't enjoy a drink with you muttering to yourself like a madwoman." From his favorite worn recliner, his gaze met mine. "What's wrong?"

I shook my head. Jack didn't need the upset. And he would be more than just upset by the bruises on my arms. *Murderous* came to mind.

Rather than admit the truth, I blurted the first thing that came to me. "I'm just worried about distribution. Are we maximizing our channels when it comes to it?"

The coarse white hair of his eyebrow rose.

Too much. Damn. Jack had always been able to read my bluffs like a skilled poker player. Which was funny since he usually lost every hand we played of Texas Hold'em. I licked my suddenly dry lips. Only one topic could dissuade him now. "Rue looked pretty last night. Don't you think?"

He snorted, his attention returning to the TV filled with explosions and gunshots. Jack liked his crime shows. I smiled, pleased my ruse had worked, until I glanced at the clock. It was too early to turn in, and too late to do much of anything in Gett. The only two bars in town would be hopping but everything else would be locked tight. I wondered what Brodie was up to at this moment. Was he searching for Marcus or had he already found him?

Maybe Brodie wouldn't do anything stupid. He was a smart guy. At least for a Gett, I thought with a grin. I paced back and forth. I didn't even realize I was doing it until Jack threw down the newspaper in his hands, storming off to his bedroom.

For a long time, I stood at the front window, staring at the darkness.

• • •

"Come on, girl," Jack called as he rushed toward the small church housing a fourth of the town of Gett. In terms of conflict, NFL games had nothing on the Gett Sunday service. For as long as I could remember, the Getts and the Luckys vied for the front pew, for less-than-pious reasons. The pew was a status symbol, worn like a badge of honor, like baking the best snickerdoodles for the Sunday social. That, and it was the only pew with a breeze blowing in from the lone open window. Seeing as the temperature had already reached eighty degrees, I couldn't fault Jack for his insistence on arriving early.

For the past nine months, he'd woken me every Sunday before the sun hit the sky in hopes of being the first to arrive at the white-walled church. We rarely were. Much too often Rue with Brodie and Danny on either side of her would shoot Jack a satisfied smirk from the coveted pew.

Every week, Pastor Matt would prattle on about sin and forgiveness. About loving thy neighbor.

And Jack would snort loudly, his glare on Rue's back.

Today proved a bit different, in that Rue sat alone in the pew, her eyes straight ahead. Jack frowned, pulling to a stop. "Wait here," he said as he headed toward the older woman, his cane barely making a sound on the highly polished wood floor.

The hairs on my arms danced as the air around me swirled. I quickly turned around. "Charlotte," Danny Gett, dressed in the industrial gray colors of the Collier County Sheriff's uniform, motioned to the *Exit* sign above the church door, "I need you to come with me."

"What? Why?"

"Please, just do what I'm asking. For once in your life."

The word *please* had me following without question. Danny wasn't the *please* or *thank you* type. Something was seriously wrong. His expression gave nothing away as I followed him out of the church, away from the prying eyes of the congregation.

I kept my mouth shut until we reached his patrol car parked on the sidewalk. "What's this all about?"

Rather than answer, he opened the door to the backseat. The scent of worn leather and fast food wafted from the vehicle, along with a hint of desperation. "Watch your head," he said as he attempted to usher me inside.

I refused to duck inside. "Am I in some kind of trouble?"

He didn't answer, just pushed the door open wider.

"Fine," I said with a growl. Bending down inside, I was surprised to find the seat made of hard plastic. The material scraped against my bare legs. I pulled down my off-the-shoulder sundress. Danny got in the driver's seat, adjusted the mirror for a long time—to avoid my questioning gaze, I suspected—and then put the car in gear.

We drove in silence for about ten minutes, long enough to cross the Gett town border and into the city of Harker. In comparison to Gett, Harker had everything, meaning a McDonald's and two stoplights. They also had the lone motel for miles around.

The same one I'd visited just yesterday.

A bad feeling welled in my throat. Had Brodie beat Marcus up and now was in trouble with the law, all because of me? I couldn't stomach the thought. "Is Brodie . . . okay?"

Putting the car into Park in the lot in front of the motel, Danny slowly turned to face me, his face a mask. "Why would you ask that?"

"I . . . ah . . ." I swallowed past the lump in my throat. "Why am I here, Danny?"

"Sheriff. Not Danny. I believe I've mentioned that before."

I frowned at the reminder of the day he questioned me for murder, and then foolishly arrested my grandfather for the crime. Danny Gett might be the sheriff of Collier County, but he wasn't an investigative mastermind. I'd be smart to remember that before I too wound up in jail. "Do I need a lawyer?"

"I'm not going to arrest you." He hesitated for the barest of seconds. "At least not yet. Unless you plan to confess?"

Confess? Confess to what? "What's going on, *Sheriff*?" The taste of his title on my lips was nearly as foul as Gett Whiskey and Diet Coke.

Before he could answer, not that he would, a flash of yellow tape on the balcony caught my eye. Crime scene tape. My gaze shot to Danny's with question. Question laced with a growing sense of alarm.

"Charlotte," he said softly, "I'm sorry to inform you of the death of your fiancé, Marcus Savage."

Chapter 10

Blood pounded in my ears, drowning out the rest of Danny's words. Was Marcus really dead? How was that even possible? I'd seen him, alive and very angry, less than twenty-four hours ago. My hand trembled, so I gripped it with my other one. "How did this happen?"

His gaze narrowed. "I'm hoping you can tell me."

I blinked. "Was he . . . murdered?"

"The investigation is ongoing." He paused. "But there was some kind of altercation, and Savage suffered blunt trauma to the head. The maid found him this morning, dead." Gazing up at the motel room door, he softly said, "He didn't suffer."

Danny wasn't a good liar. My stomach lurched.

"Can you answer a few questions?"

"I didn't do this," I yelped.

He gave me a small smile. "If you say so." He motioned to the crime scene hidden behind the motel room wall. "Whoever killed him . . . they were very angry."

My mind flashed to Brodie and the sound of his retreating boots on the driveway last night. "No, it couldn't be."

"Couldn't be who, Charlotte?" His voice took on a soothing tone. "Do you know who's responsible?"

"Of course not," I said, even as Brodie's stark face from the night before filled my vision. If I told Danny the truth about Brodie, he'd only cover up his brother's involvement. It was the Gett way. Just like the incident with the water tower. Danny knew Brodie had painted it, and yet, he let everyone think it was me.

"When did you talk to Savage last?" he asked, voice edged with ice.

"Yesterday morning. Here. Maybe ten."

"And that was the last time?"

I nodded.

"Seems odd for a newly engaged couple . . ."

"We weren't engaged," I blurted.

His gaze fell to that damn ring on my finger. "Is that so?"

I tucked my hand further under my arm. "Yes. That's what we . . . talked about."

He nodded, as if the pieces fell in place. "He broke it off, and that made you angry. Didn't it?" Running the back of his hand along the edge of his chin, his gaze never left my face.

My head jerked up. "You *do* think I killed him!"

"I didn't say that."

I snorted. "Well, I didn't. I was at the distillery all day yesterday, and then at home all night."

"With Jack?"

My brows snapped together. "You can't honestly believe a man in his seventies won a fight with a man forty years younger."

Danny frowned. "Jack's feisty."

"Yes, he was at home all night with me." If he thought he could pin another murder rap on my grandfather, Danny Gett was seriously mistaken. Especially when, in my mind, right now his own brother was the best, if not only, suspect.

"That's her, Sheriff," an older woman I didn't recognize, her gray hair piled high on top her head, declared in a screech.

Danny opened his door and got out to speak to the woman. What did she mean when she said, *that's her*? I stared at the woman, trying to remember her face. Through the slight crack in the window, I heard her say, "She said that he'd be sorry, and that she'd make sure of it."

"I did not!" I yelled from the backseat of the police car, which, all in all, wasn't the greatest place to declare one's innocence.

The woman gave me a good frown, and I wasn't sure if it was for interrupting her big moment or my denial. "Yes, she most certainly did. I heard her with my very own ears."

Danny turned to me, his dark eyebrow hitched. "Is that so?"

"I said no such thing." But Marcus had. His harsh threat came flooding back and I shivered in the heat of the squad car. I had nothing to fear from him anymore, I reminded myself. Someone had made sure of that. Once again, Brodie came to mind.

Clearing my throat, I demanded, "Either arrest me or take me home."

Danny appeared to consider both options, much longer than I liked. Finally, he flagged one of his deputies over, ordering him to drive me home. Danny's eyes bore into mine for a long moment. "See you real soon, Charlotte."

He tapped the top of the car and the deputy put it into gear, slowly pulling away. Danny's gaze stayed locked on mine. I fought the urge to squirm, and instead gave him a wide smile and a wave.

Chapter 11

Minutes later, the deputy, at my insistence, dropped me off in front of Brodie's single-room house on the outskirts of Gett. White paint flaked from the exterior, falling into the window box below filled with wilted yellow flowers. For some inexplicable reason the sight brought wetness to my eyes. Now was not the time to grieve. Justice was needed far more than my tears.

I rapped on Brodie's front door, the engagement ring on my finger glinting in the sunlight. "Open up." I smacked my fist into the wood again.

Mrs. Branson, Brodie's neighbor and queen of the local gossips, peeked her head over the side of her porch. Her one good eye focused on me, widening. I knocked again. Quieter this time.

Footsteps sounded, and a few seconds later the door squeaked open. Brodie stuck his head out. He yanked the door all the way open when he saw me. "Charms? What are you doing here?"

Now that I found myself on his doorstep I wasn't sure what to say. Outright accusing him of murder sounded rude at best, especially with Mrs. Branson listening to our every word. I swallowed hard, until I noticed the dark circle around his eye. The same size as a man's fist. "How could you!"

Eyes darting to Mrs. Branson, and back to me, he grabbed my hands, dragging me into his house. I started to scream but he slapped his palm over my mouth. I slammed my foot into the top of his bare foot. He didn't even flinch. When the front door closed behind me with an ominous click he let me go, taking a step back. "How could I what?" he asked, voice calm and collected. The kind of tone cops used to talk people from bridges.

I took immediate offense. "Don't you dare talk to me like I'm crazy."

"Okaaaay," he said with a quick grin as he held up his hand and backed slowly away.

I guess I did sound a little crazed. Even if he had killed Marcus, the odds of him deciding to end my existence were slim at best. "How did you get that black eye?" I asked rather accuse him of murder. I'd save that for later. When I had a bunch of non-Gett police backup.

Touching the darkened skin under his eye, he met my gaze. "I fell."

"I see. Any chance you fell into Marcus's fist?"

"Who told you that?"

"Lucky guess." My shoulders slumped. So it was true. Brodie had gone to Marcus to defend me and Marcus ended up dead. Guilt overwhelmed me. "Why didn't you call 9-1-1?"

He snorted. "You're kidding, right?"

I recoiled from the coldness of his words. I hadn't truly believed him capable of such heartlessness, not the boy I used to know. But this man standing before me . . . he could kill without blinking an eye. "I think you should get a lawyer," I said, slipping around him and to the door. My fingers closed on the knob, but his next words stalled my hand.

"Marcus is pressing charges? Figures." He snorted. "Charms, he hit me. I barely touched the guy."

"Barely touched him?" I spun around. "You killed him!"

"Whoa." He held up a hand, staggering back. "What are you talking about?"

"Marcus," I said softly. "He's dead."

He took another step backward. "I . . . what happened?"

Did he really not know? Was it possible Marcus hadn't died right away after they fought? I stared at him for a long moment before speaking. "Danny dragged me from church this morning to the Harker Motel, where a maid found Marcus's body."

He blew out a breath. "That's good news."

"What?!" My anger blazed. A man was dead, and Brodie was likely going to end up in prison for ten to life. How could he be so cavalier?

He winced. "Relax, Charms. I only meant it's good that he was at the Harker Motel."

"Why? What does that matter?"

"Come inside." He waved me to his cozy kitchen. "I'll make some coffee and tell you all about it."

Chapter 12

I sat at Brodie's kitchen table, a cup of freshly brewed coffee cupped in my hands. He poured a cup for himself, and then sat too. We drank the caffeinated brew in silence. Once my cup was half empty, I lifted my gaze to his. "Okay, let's hear it."

He nodded, setting his cup down. His finger, long with just a hint of dark hair below the knuckle, traced the cypress wood tabletop for a long moment before he spoke. "I wasn't at the Harker Motel last night. So whatever happened there wasn't my doing."

"But you did fight with him?"

He ducked his head as if unable to meet my eyes. "If you could call it a fight. The guy sucker punched me at the Gett. Willow jumped in between us before I took my own shot." He hesitated, his eyes drifting to my shoulders and the welts hidden under my shirt. "All of this was before I knew anything about those bruises." His lips curved into a glower. "Believe me, had I known, the outcome would've been quite different."

"You never hit him?"

"Not really."

I frowned. "That's not a no."

"I shoved him." Shoulders lifting into a shrug, he added, "Nothing more."

Taking another sip of the now lukewarm coffee, I hesitated to ask, "Why?"

"Why what?" he asked, again not meeting my eyes.

"You know exactly what I'm asking. What were you fighting about?"

He stood, pacing the small but inviting kitchen nook. Surprisingly, everything in Brodie's house looked cozy and comfortable, with plenty of wood accents and brown leather. They suited him perfectly. Finally, he stopped, his gaze hard on mine. "It's not important, Charms. Trust me on this."

It was my turn to look away. "I wish I could."

He eased back into his chair. "Do you really think that I killed him?"

I stared into his eyes for a long moment, unsure how to answer.

Some people claim that the eyes are a window to the soul, but in Brodie's case, his indigo-colored gaze gave nothing away. "It's not important," I repeated his earlier words. "What matters is what the rest of the town believes."

"How so?"

"By now everyone knows about the fight you and Marcus had." I ran my finger over the rim of the cup. "It's not a far leap for people to draw the same conclusion that I did."

He laughed, and then sobered, shaking his head. "No one around here, with the exception of you, would think that I had anything to do with his death."

I raised an eyebrow. "Is that so? What about outside Gett? Once word gets to the tabloids, and it will get out, you'll be their top suspect. Convicted in print before the Gett money can rush in to save you."

He winced. "You do have a point. What do you suggest I do about it?"

"I suggest *we* give them another suspect."

"Danny's not going to like us interfering in another of his investigations."

Probably not, but I really didn't care. Though my relationship with Marcus had ended badly, I wasn't about to let a murderer get away with such a despicable act. Nor would I allow myself or Brodie to take the fall for another's crime. "I have a feeling Danny would like you in prison even less."

"That makes two of us," he said with a laugh.

"Three."

He tilted his head, his familiar cocky smirk firmly in place. "I didn't know you cared."

I snorted, loud and unladylike.

Once again, he stood, his body ridged. "All kidding aside, Charms, I don't think you should get involved."

My eyes narrowed. "Excuse me?"

His hand rose, and then fell to his side. "Don't get huffy. I'm just . . ."

"What?" I bit out. "Afraid for little ole me?"

"How much bloodshed can I expect if I say yes?"

I shrugged. "No more than a pint, I'm sure. But, before you

take your life into your own hands, let me say, I *am* involved. Marcus was here because of me. I owe it to—"

Brodie interrupted before I could finish. "Was he?"

"Was he what?"

He licked his lips. "How do you know that Savage was here because of you? Maybe he had another reason . . ."

"Which means . . ." I paused, the guilt I'd felt since this morning easing a bit, "someone else might've had a reason to want him dead."

"Exactly."

Chapter 13

Brodie and I spent the next hour trying to figure out what other possible reasons Marcus had for coming to Gett. It wasn't like he was hanging around in order to catch the eye of a movie producer or studio executive. The closest Gett had was George Rampart, who filmed himself driving his riding lawnmower off the roof of his eighty-seven-year-old mother's house last month after drinking a twelve-pack of beer. Sadly, for our investigation as well as for his mother, George was still in a full body cast.

"What about Evan?" Brodie asked suddenly.

As the denial formed on my lips, I bit it back. While I couldn't believe Evan would kill Marcus, or anyone for that matter, he did know him. Maybe better than I thought. "A possibility. But why would he kill him? What motive would he have?"

"You," he said.

"How so?"

He shrugged. "The bruises. Maybe Evan saw them . . ."

I couldn't help but laugh. "Evan would applaud him, not kill him. In case you didn't figure it out, Evan and I are not that close. He's tried more than once to convince me I belong in Hollywood, not Gett. In fact, I'd bet he would like to see me in a body bag long before Marcus."

"I'd heard something to that effect but couldn't believe it."

When he didn't say more, my eyebrow rose in anticipation. "And why is that?"

"Who wouldn't find you absolutely charming?"

I rolled my eyes. "You're hilarious. Can we get back to finding a killer?"

He shrugged. "If we must."

Thirty minutes later, our suspect list was still at one—cousin Evan.

I stared at the piece of paper with his name written in Brodie's scrawled handwriting and tried to control the butterflies in my stomach. Jack would be devastated if Evan was guilty. Heck, I might even shed a tear. Blood was blood, after all.

"Charms," Brodie said, gaining my attention. "Evan is probably innocent."

"I know."

He snatched the paper from in front of me, balled it up, and threw it in the trash. "I have . . . some stuff to do today, but tonight, we'll talk to Evan. Okay?"

"All right," I said, rising from the chair and heading for the door, only mildly curious what sort of *stuff* Brodie had to do today. And would he be doing that stuff to Mindy Drift? The two of them had looked chummy at Jack's party. I hesitated at the door, wanting to ask him despite my better judgment.

Thankfully a violent pounding on the wood interrupted my impulse. Brodie shoved me behind his back, throwing the door wide to confront the threat. Danny Gett stood on the other side, his fist raised to knock again. When he saw his brother his face relaxed, and then his eyes went to me. "You've got to be kidding me," he said in a growl. Danny pushed his way inside, saying, "We've got to talk."

From behind him, a flash of bright light caught my eye, blinding me for a second. I blinked until the streaks of silver light faded from my vision. "Damn," Brodie whispered just as a bald man with a large camera around his neck ran toward us, screaming, "Ms. Lucky, is there any truth to the rumors of your affair with Brodie Gett?"

I froze, like a deer in the headlights of an oncoming semitruck. I could do nothing to stop the rising sense of inevitability. And then came the question that sealed our fate.

"Did you kill your fiancé so the two of you could be together?"

Chapter 14

Brodie yanked me back inside. My legs felt weak, and I stumbled. Before I fell, he caught me in his arms. The camera whirled, capturing it all. Danny kicked the door closed. "How the hell did that miscreant learn Savage is dead?" he mumbled. "We haven't even released his name yet."

"Why not?" I asked, trying to get over the shock of the paparazzo's questions. Did the cameraman really not only think I had something to do with Marcus's death but that Brodie was my secret lover? The whole idea was laughable until one realized Marcus was indeed dead.

For a moment Danny didn't answer, and when he did, I wished he hadn't. "We're trying to notify his next of kin, but so far, no luck."

When we were dating in Hollywood, Marcus had rarely spoken about his childhood, or his family. I did remember he mentioned having a sister. I said as much to Danny. "Do you remember her name?" he asked, taking out his notebook.

"Deane, I think."

"Deane Savage. Got it." His pen scratched against the notebook.

"No," I said quickly.

"But you just said exactly that," he growled. He threw up his hands, mumbling about women, particularly one unlucky one. I stifled a smile as he muttered to himself. "What I meant to say was, Savage isn't . . . wasn't Marcus's real surname. He made it up when he arrived in Hollywood."

Danny's face tensed when I didn't say more. "So what was his real name?"

For some bizarre reason, giving him Marcus's real name felt like an invasion, like I was betraying Marcus somehow. Which was ridiculous. The man was dead, and the sooner his family was notified, the sooner they could begin to process the senseless event. Plus, it would be awful if his relatives learned of his murder on *TMZ*. "Smellie," I said. "Marcus Smellie."

"Right," Danny said, and then turned around as if to examine a speck of dirt on Brodie's far wall. Brodie seemed to suddenly develop an interest in his hardwood floor, for his eyes stayed locked on the ground. I blew out a sharp breath. "Are you thirteen-year-old boys? Yes. His name was Smellie. It doesn't mean he stunk. Get over it."

Danny nodded. "Some people are just born with very misleading surnames."

Brodie held up his hand before I could respond. "Sorry. You're right, Charms."

I nodded, slightly mollified, though hating the easy way my nickname rolled off his tongue. "Danny," Brodie said, "what brings you by?" As if he didn't already know.

The sheriff gave me a pointed look. Brodie shrugged in silent communication, like Gett Morse code, filled with long pauses and awkward shrugging. "I'm guessing you heard about Savage," Danny finally said to his brother.

Brodie nodded but didn't comment.

Tugging at the collar of his shirt, Danny continued, "Do you have something to tell me?"

"Not really. Why? What do you think you know?"

"You and Savage got into an altercation a few hours before his death."

Brodie's face hardened. "Willow promised not to say anything. Damn her."

Danny took a menacing step toward his brother, his gaze hot enough to distill whiskey without a still. "Willow didn't break her word. How could you think she would? She's practically family." He shook his head. "Horace Kerry was there. He saw the whole thing."

Horace was one of Danny's deputies. Of course he'd tell the sheriff about the fight. I stepped between the two men before the famous Gett temper exploded. "I'm sure Brodie didn't mean anything by it. He just knows how close you and Willow are."

Brodie tensed behind me. "I can speak for myself, Charms."

"Then do it," I bit out. We needed Danny on our side, especially since he was likely to feel extreme pressure to make an arrest.

Brodie grinned, the tension fading from his body. "Danny," he began, "I—"

"Forget it." He waved his brother's apology off. "Tell me about the fight. Horace said Savage struck first."

"He did."

"That's good. Real good." Danny ran a hand through his dark hair. Beyond Brodie's closed front door, more questions were shouted by the lone cameraman. I winced as the questions turned to harsh, ugly accusations. Danny sighed when the man screamed the word *cover-up*. "Why couldn't Savage get himself killed in Hollywood."

My spine tightened, but I held my tongue.

"Get rid of that guy and I'll answer all your questions, all right?" Brodie said to his brother.

Danny's eyes narrowed, as if he didn't quite believe his sibling. "You'd better." With that, he walked past me and out the door, shutting it behind him. Danny's stern voice rang out as he ordered the cameraman to disburse. For a moment, I actually hoped the man wouldn't comply, thereby forcing Danny to use force. The more excessive the better. As soon as the horrible thought crossed my mind, I shook it away.

"Okay, Charms, let's go find ourselves a killer," Brodie declared, waving to his patio door and the swamp beyond. A worn dirt path cut through it, connecting Brodie's house to almost all of Gett, including the Lucky property.

I swallowed, memories of my own near-death encounter a few months ago in the same swamp rising forefront in my mind. I didn't want to be gator chow and I especially didn't want to be gator food while wearing a thong. Jack would die of shock when the cops retrieved my body.

As if Brodie could read my mind, that damn familiar smirk filled his lips.

"Oh, do shut up," I said, blowing out a pent-up breath before rushing headlong down the path.

Chapter 15

Brodie and I walked along the path in silence. Swamp water churned as something big and brown ducked beneath the surface of the brackish water inches away. Instinctively I leapt backward, crashing into Brodie. He wrapped his arms around me to steady me, or maybe to stop me from running away, screaming. I was betting on the latter.

Once my heartbeat calmed to around a hundred and sixty beats per minute, I pulled away from him, giving him a good frown. Blustering my way through my embarrassment seemed like a good idea. "Do you mind?"

He snorted. "Charms, it's a good thing you gave up acting."

"Hey!"

Without another word, he grabbed my hand and started down the narrow muddy path again. People in Gett, especially those who lived along the swamp like Brodie, all had a path like this one. A way to get from one place to another in half the time, if you wanted to risk life and most often limb. I opted for saner routes, avoiding stray gators with foot and other limb fetishes.

Halfway to the Lucky family grounds the mangrove trees closed in around us along with hanging vines, turning the bright Florida sun murky. The air hung heavily, doing nothing to dispel the scent of wet earth and rotting foliage. Goose bumps rose on my arms. I ran my hand up my skin to ward off the chill.

"Are you cold?" Brodie asked, and not in a gentlemanly tone. He sounded both surprised and amused by the possibility. I went from feeling grateful for his presence to wanting to push him into the muddy water.

I shot him a glare. "Considering my blood isn't half whiskey like your own, yes, I'm a little chilled." As the words came out of my lips, I wanted to swallow them back. If Brodie wanted to spend all his time at a bar, that was his business. Not mine.

"Ouch," he said with a grin, his hand moving to his chest. "I'm wounded."

And he had been. Not very long ago. My mind flashed to the angry red scars on his chest. The one's that nearly killed him in a far-off war zone. I couldn't let him risk his life again, not to help me find Marcus's killer. "This isn't going to work."

"What?"

I motioned between us. "This. Us."

His eyebrow rose. "Are you breaking up with me?"

"You're hilarious. Really," I said. "But you know exactly what I'm talking about. It's a bad idea for us to investigate Marcus's death."

"Why?"

"Because . . ." I frowned, unable to think of a reason Brodie would accept, ". . . if we're seen together, it will make things worse."

"No."

"What do you mean, no?" I yanked on his arm so he'd pull to a stop. He didn't, so instead I nearly landed flat on my face. For the second time in as many minutes, he steadied me in his arms. I hated both needing his help and how much I enjoyed the warmth radiating from his body. I was colder than I thought.

He grinned down at me. "No means just that, Charms. I don't agree with you, nor am I about to let you go off by yourself to investigate Savage's murder. I made that mistake once before, and you almost ended up dead. So, no matter how much you piss me off, I'm sticking to you like glue. Which is what I'm assuming is in the Lucky Whiskey recipe."

I shoved away from him. "There's no reasoning with a Gett."

"Got that right."

"Fine." I stomped away, toward the Lucky Distillery. "Know this, Brodie Gett. When this blows up in our faces, and it surely will, I'm going to get immense pleasure in saying *I told you so* over and over again."

"So what you're saying is," he said to my back, "it will be like any other day."

• • •

A few minutes later, we stepped from the underbrush and onto the land my family had owned for generations. A stream, the lifeblood of Lucky Whiskey, divided the property in half. The water looked fresh and clear, at odds with the swamp water a hundred feet away, and the mixed emotions swirling inside me.

"Looks like Jack's home," I said, weaving around the vehicle in the driveway. Since Danny had pulled me from church this morning, Jack had been left to his own devices, which likely included a glass of whiskey and bacon. "I think we should keep him in the dark about Marcus's death for now. It will only upset him."

Brodie snorted. "I doubt it."

"Do you have to argue with me about everything?"

"It would seem so." He grinned. "Look at that, we finally agree on something."

"Just do me a favor and don't say anything about Marcus. Not yet." When he nodded, I gave him a smile, then headed for the front door of the Lucky house. Brodie trailed behind me. I opened the door, walking in without knocking as I'd done my entire life.

A mistake.

One I regretted instantly when I saw Jack and Rue Gett jump apart like teenagers caught hooking up. Thankfully I hadn't actually witnessed any kissing or worse, for the sight would've scarred me for life.

"Char, girl," Jack said with a frown. "Where have you . . ." His words fell off as Brodie walked in the house behind me. "Jack," Brodie said with a tilt of his head. His eyes widened when he saw his grandmother. "Rue? What are you doing here?"

The older woman visibly stiffened. "What you should be asking is for my forgiveness."

Under his breath, he muttered something intelligible before asking the obvious. "Forgiveness for what?"

Her cane tapped on the ground. "Stand up straight when you talk to me, boy."

If Brodie's spine got any straighter it would surely snap, so what was her game?

"You promised to take me to church this morning. I called last night to make sure, but you never answered." She gave him a hard frown. "If it wasn't for Jack, I'd have had no way home. Not with Danny standing me up as well. When did you boys become so disrespectful?"

Brodie looked instantly contrite. "I'm sorry. I forgot."

I hid a smile. Rue wielded guilt like others did a weapon.

One of her white eyebrows arched. "Is that so?"

A blush bloomed on his cheeks. "I . . . had a late night."

"With that Drift girl? I though the two of you looked chummy at my birthday party," Jack said. "Up until Moore took a dive into the cake."

"I wasn't with Mindy."

If he wasn't with Mindy, just where had he been? The yellow crime scene tape from this morning flashed through my brain. I swallowed hard.

"Thank you, Jack, for bringing Rue here." He hesitated, his face paling as he glanced between them. As if he too suspected something torrid going on. Or as torrid as one could get without breaking a hip. "Why exactly are you here instead of at home?"

Now it was Rue's turn to pale. As quickly as she lost color, it returned, with vengeance. Twin blooms of redness exploded under the rouge carefully applied to her cheeks. "What do you think we're doing! We were waiting for Charlotte, of course. We wanted to be here to comfort her."

"Comfort me?" I repeated. Somehow, not unsurprisingly, Jack and Rue had already learned of Marcus's death. I hoped the news hadn't yet spread to the rest of the town, especially the rumors of the affair between Brodie and me.

Rue rose to her feet with the use of her cane. "We heard . . . about your fiancé's death, dear. You don't have to be brave for us."

Jack seconded her sentiment by wrapping his arms around me, pulling me to him, while smacking me in the back. While I appreciated the attempt, it felt like he'd dislodged my right lung with his ministrations. Brodie must've recognized my peril, for he separated us with a few words. "Charms is just fine. In fact, she's lucky that piece of . . . dirt is dead."

Jack's face reddened. "Boy, have some respect. The love of Char's life just died. This isn't time for jealousy."

Brodie opened his mouth to defend himself, but Rue smacked his shin with her cane before he could speak. She then turned on Jack, taking a threatening step toward him. Which, to an outsider, might've seemed ridiculous. This tiny eighty-year-old woman dressed in her Sunday best, standing up to a man who towered over her, even with his stooped shoulders.

But we all knew better.

Rue was formidable, and as Brodie could attest to, dangerous with that wooden cane. "Don't you speak to my grandson like that." When Jack looked less than contrite, she took another menacing step toward him. He stared at her for a long moment, and then nodded. That seemed to satisfy her, for she turned her wrath on the very grandson she'd sought to protect. "Brodie, you were raised better than that. Apologize to Charlotte right this instant."

"Hold on," I said. "Why did you call Marcus the love of my life?" I thought Jack knew me better than that. Brodie shot me a quick, knowing grin. "Say one word and I'll ask your grandmother to crack you in the shin again," I whispered to him before facing Jack again.

A frown wrinkled Rue's forehead. "You agreeing to marry him sent a strong message, dear."

"You wouldn't have said yes unless you loved the man and planned to make a life with him in California." Jack looked just as confused as Rue by the question.

Brodie gazed at the ring on my finger, nodding.

Rather than explain how I'd managed to get myself accidentally engaged, I turned on my heel and headed for the kitchen. The ring felt ten times heavier with each step. I pulled at it, with no luck. It refused to budge no matter how hard I tugged.

Yanking the water faucet to icy cold, I held my hand under the spray until every nerve in my hand revolted. Only then did I give the ring another tug. I added a growl of frustration when it stayed in place and pulled harder. My skin grew raw under the pressure.

Without a word, Brodie turned off the water and dried my hand with the nearest towel. He held my cold fingers in the warmth of his hand for a long moment, his gaze locked on the ring.

"It won't come off," I said inanely.

"I can see that." Taking my hand, he moved to the ancient refrigerator against the far wall. He pulled it open, removing a container of plant-based margarine, the bane of Jack's existence since his heart attack. A smile grew on his lips. "No wonder why Jack's always begging me to bring over a pound of bacon."

"Don't you dare," I yelped.

The grin increased to a full laugh. "I wouldn't dare."

I wasn't sure I believed him, but I let it go, seeing as he was swirling the buttery substitute along my ring finger. The gesture was intimate, so much so I took an awkward step back, running into the countertop. He followed, his hand gripping mine like a lifeline. "Relax, Charms. You want this thing off, right?"

For a moment, I had no idea what thing he meant. Then it all came roaring back. Marcus was dead. Murdered. And everyone, including my own grandfather, thought we'd been engaged. "Is it working?" I asked when Brodie eased the tip of his finger along the edge of the ring to loosen it.

He bit his lip. "I don't want to hurt you."

"I wouldn't let you." The words sounded hollow to my ears; however, Brodie failed to notice.

The ring stayed in place, much to my dismay and Brodie's apparent disgust, for he frowned at it for what seemed like an eternity. Finally, he shook his head, stepping away. I grabbed a towel from the counter, wiping away the butter substitute. The scent of chemicals and oils wafted from my hand, reminding me of my missed breakfast at the Gett Diner. Jack and I always went to the diner after church. He would order bacon and eggs while I listed every artery-clogging component. Just back from maternity leave, Cindy Mae would eventually throw up her arms and storm off, only to return with egg substitutes and soy bacon. Jack would spend the entire meal glaring at me.

How I missed it. And not because my stomach grumbled, again reminding me of the lack of breakfast. Brodie's grin told me he'd heard it too. My chin tilted higher, daring him to mention it. He didn't, for which I was thankful. "Charms," he said, "I better get back to Danny before he arrests me just for ticking him off."

I nodded, though I didn't want him to leave. For his sake. Who knew what lurked outside the safety of the Lucky house. There was a killer on the loose, after all.

"Tonight, I'll pick you up and we'll go see what Evan knows about any of this." He set the margarine back in the fridge. From behind the door he said, "In the meantime, stay inside with the door locked. Promise me, Charms."

"I promise," I said, my fingers childishly crossed behind my back. There was no time to lose. The longer Marcus's true killer went unmasked, the more sensationalized his murder would get. And that wouldn't bode well for Brodie, or better yet, myself.

Chapter 16

I spent the next hour assuring Rue and Jack that I was doing all right after receiving the news of Marcus's death. Even so, Jack wouldn't let up on what he considered consoling me. Which included his pounding me on the back at random intervals. I knew he meant well, but I'd have even more bruises at this rate. Thankfully, I'd convinced Rue I didn't need a box of tissue and a gallon of ice cream. I needed to get out of the house, for my sanity's sake if not to start my investigation, so I offered to drive Rue home.

Somehow I'd managed to avoid yet another of Jack's back slaps as I helped Rue into Jack's rusted Ford. One day soon, the insurance check from my wrecked Prius would come and I could buy something from this century, but until then, Jack had, a bit unwillingly, let me drive his beloved truck. The thing had so many rust spots I worried my feet would crash through the floorboard when I applied the brakes.

"Take it easy on the clutch, girl," he warned.

"I will," I vowed, for the hundredth time. Carefully I stepped down on the pedal, and cranked the gear into reverse. I'd learned to drive in this very vehicle what felt like a lifetime ago. So much had changed, and yet had stayed the exact same.

Rue and I set out toward her estate three miles away. We drove in silence, because the radio had died a decade earlier, until she broke it. "Can I ask you a question, dear?"

I nodded, keeping my eyes on the road.

"Jack thinks you'll leave Gett once he's back on his feet."

Nine months ago, I was dying to get back to LA, but now, I wasn't so sure. There was something to be said for the slower pace of life in Gett. And for family. Jack loved me, unconditionally. He was my blood. My only relative, at least the only one I liked. While I loved my cousin Evan, because genetics said I had to, I didn't like him. Not in the least. He was an entitled brat, leeching off Jack. Yet another reason to stick around Gett once Jack was back to whiskey business. Otherwise, Evan would bleed Jack and the business dry again.

When I didn't respond, she added, "Is he right?"

I shrugged. Discussing my departure with a business rival didn't sit right, at least not until I talked with Jack. And only if and when I knew the answer for myself.

"Your being here keeps Jack on the right track," she said. "Not that he'd admit it. Men, my dear, are stubborn, often foolish creatures. It's best to let them think they're in charge. But we know better."

I swallowed a laugh. I'd bet Rue knew this better than anyone, as she was surrounded by the personification of the stubborn males, from her son to his offspring. Each thought they knew what was best for her, for the whiskey, but she was the true guiding force behind it all. I respected her for it, even as her controlling, competitive nature drove Jack nuts. "I have no intention of making any decisions about my future until Jack's fully recovered."

"Good."

The single word bothered me. It was as if I'd given her more of an answer than I knew for myself. "Right. Good," I parroted. A minute later, I pulled into the perfect, unpitted blacktop drive of the Gett estate. The house loomed in front of me, the white façade glaringly brightly in the Florida sun. I suspect it could be seen from space.

Marshall, dressed in a charcoal-colored suit, opened the front door. His dark hair, streaked with gray, contrasted against the brightness of the house. I gave him a wave. His lips split into a wide smile as he waved back. He came down the porch steps to help Rue down. She patted my arm, thanked me for the ride, and used her cane to make her way into the house. Marshall hung back.

My eyebrow rose in question.

He waited until Rue cleared the entryway before speaking. "A stranger with a camera has been spotted at the front gate of the distillery. I didn't want to upset Rue with the news, but I'm worried it has something to do with the rumors swirling about."

For as long as I could remember, Marshall had worked for the Getts. He called himself a manservant, but he was much more. He ran the household, seeing to Rue's needs, as well as to her security. No one stepped foot on the Gett estate, let alone the distillery, without Marshall knowing it.

I'd learned this lesson the hard way when I'd managed to

sneak inside the five-car garage behind the house a few months ago. Marshall didn't say a word about my breaking and entering as he served me dinner later that evening. Instead, I found a nicely penned note along with a box of the best chocolate chip cookies I'd ever tasted in the mailbox a month later. It thanked me for solving the murder of Roger Kerrick, and also suggested I ask next time before breaking into a Gett property.

Since then, Marshall and I had developed an odd sort of friendship, based on a shared love of cookies, and my inability to bake a single one without ruining it. He'd kindly offered to cater Jack's birthday party along with Sweet Jayme. Sadly the party, which would've gone down in Gett history for the delicious food alone, would now be remembered mostly for Jonas Moore's untimely death.

And also my doomed one-day engagement.

I swallowed before asking in the most innocent of tones, "Rumors?"

He rolled his eyes. "That act might work on someone else, but you know exactly what I'm talking about. Rue will have a fit when she hears them."

"I know." I sagged against the fabric of the driver's seat. Years of stale cigar smoke wafted around me.

Marshall kindly didn't bat an eye. "I'll try to keep her from hearing the worst of it, but you need to fix this and fast, before the Gett name is dragged through the mud."

I didn't bother to ask why he didn't mention the Lucky name. We'd been muddy since long before I was born. "Thank you. And thank you again for helping with Jack's birthday. The food was amazing." My stomach grumbled at the memory of slathered ribs and corn so sweet it almost tasted like sugar pops. I still hadn't eaten breakfast, and now I'd also missed lunch. My hands started to shake when I thought about my next meal. I gripped the steering wheel to stop the telling action.

"Speaking of which," he said, "can you do me a favor since I don't want to leave Rue alone with that menace with the camera about?"

"Of course."

"I made a brisket and sweet corn casserole for Grace Moore."

"That's kind of you."

He shrugged. "Least I could do. Poor woman. She's much too young to be a widow. Would you mind driving it over to her?"

"Not at all," I said. The Moores' house wasn't too far and would take me right past the starting point of my investigation— the Gett Bar & Grill. It was the last place I knew of that anyone saw or spoke with Marcus, except for his killer.

With a smile, Marshall turned on his heel and headed back into the house. A few minutes later he was back, a glass dish in his hands. Foil covered the top. But it was no match for the heavenly scent drifting from it. My mouth watered as the smoky aroma reached my nose. My stomach grumble grew to unprecedented heights. I grabbed a stick of gum from the pack on the dashboard to stop myself from diving into the dish entrusted to me for safe delivery.

He thanked me and then disappeared back into the house. I put the truck in gear, my eyes straight ahead, for I dared not look at the foil-covered glass. It didn't stop my stomach from constantly reminding me of the gooey goodness lurking inches away.

Chapter 17

I drove past the Gett Bar & Grill, surprised to see the dirt lot void of vehicles, until I remembered it was Sunday. The Lord's day. Here in Gett that meant no alcohol sold, and all bars were closed. This was unheard of in the rest of the county, and much of the state. And yet, no one questioned the decree in Gett.

The Moores lived outside town, in what many considered the grass-is-greener part. Which I had to agree with, as the lawns of the few newer houses were actually a much deeper emerald color than those in town. However, the streets were far from paved in gold. In fact, they weren't paved at all. I bumped along the gravel road to the Moores' property, my teeth rattling with each rut.

I followed Route 105 until the Moores' large house came into view. *Large* wasn't an exaggeration. In a town where most homes averaged about a thousand square feet, the Moores' house was five times that. Though it wasn't nearly as big as the Gett estate.

Rolling down the window, I stuck my head halfway out, breathing in air that wasn't tinged with brisket and sweet corn casserole. I promised my stomach a meal at the Gett Diner as soon as I dropped the casserole off for Grace.

I pulled into the long driveway, parked, and got out, the dish securely in my hands. And surprisingly not missing a single bite. I made my way to the front door, knocking on the bleached oak door. My knock sounded hollow, like the house was alone and grieving too. I shifted the dish from hand to hand while I waited for Grace to answer.

After thirty seconds or so, I peered through the glass inserts around the front door. The warped reflection offered little insight into the goings-on beyond. Grace was probably off making arrangements for her husband's funeral. How terrible she must feel. I couldn't imagine her pain. When my own parents had died, I'd been too young to understand that they wouldn't be coming back to tuck me in at night. Thankfully though I'd had Jack. While his bed-tucking skills were lacking he'd loved me like his own child.

Shaking off my morose thoughts, I headed back to the truck to search for a pen and paper so I could leave a note along with the casserole. Luck was on my side when I found a pencil, the kind used to keep score and/or cheat at putt-putt, tucked under the driver's seat. A smile filled my face, remembering Jack and I playing the extreme putt-putt in Naples for my twelfth birthday. I'd won by three strokes.

It took me a few more minutes to find a suitable piece of paper. My options ranged from a questionably crumpled tissue to a foil gum wrapper. Wisely, I opted for the foil paper. I scribbled a note for Grace and left it along with the casserole on her front porch.

Did gators like sweet corn casserole? I hoped not. In case they did, I moved it up to the porch railing. Once I was satisfied the casserole would be safe, from my hunger at least, I hopped back into the worn bench seat of the pickup, cranked it into gear with only a mild squeal, and drove down the road until I arrived at the Gett Diner.

• • •

Twenty minutes later, I sucked on the paper straw swirling in my sweet tea, enjoying the coating of sugar on my tongue. If my Hollywood friends could see me now. I'd gone more native than I'd thought. Nine months ago, I'd have ordered salad, worrying incessantly about the circumference of my thighs. These days I ate with taste rather than body image in mind.

"Eating your feelings?" Cindy Mae asked.

I shook my head, smiling at the blond woman, her eyelids creased from sleepless nights. A few weeks ago she'd birthed a baby boy named Cole. He was cute in the way babies were to those uninterested in having one of their own. "Nope, just soaking up the atmosphere," I replied. As much as I liked Cindy Mae, she had a habit of gossiping. I didn't need to add fuel to any of the rumors already swirling.

"Meeting someone?" she asked.

My brow rose as I glanced pointedly at the second menu on the table across from me.

"Right." She gave a small laugh. "What I meant to say is, *who* are you meeting?"

Willow Jones, dressed in her standard uniform of T-shirt and jeans, saved me from answering as she strolled through the front door and headed our way, her copper-colored hair barely contained by a ponytail. She gave me a small wave as she approached.

Cindy Mae's face fell. "Oh."

I stifled a laugh. She'd expected Brodie to be my guest. I took pleasure in her disappointment. Willow must've recognized the look in Cindy Mae's eyes, as she spent plenty of time on the Gett gossip list, for she asked about Cole as a means of distracting Cindy Mae. Or maybe she really was interested in the color of the baby's bowel movements.

After Cindy Mae left, Willow's drink orders on the pad of paper in her hand and a happy smile on her lips, Willow looked pointedly my way. "Not that I don't appreciate the invitation, but I'm guessing you don't want to just chat about the weather."

"True."

Her voice lowered to a whisper. "Is this about what happened to your fiancé?"

Before I could respond, Cindy Mae was back, her hands holding another sweet tea for Willow. "Know what you want? I suggest the fish and chips, as Manny caught the crappie fresh this morning."

Willow took her up on the offer, but I declined, instead ordering a slice of bourbon apple pie. Cindy Mae walked to the counter that separated the kitchen from the diners. A large metal order wheel spun clockwise between the waitstaff and Manny, the cook. Only four other diners sat scattered around the tables, awaiting their meals. Though all eyes were on me.

Rather than explain to Willow about my accidental engagement to a now dead man, I licked my lips and said, "In a way." Picking up the thin paper napkin in front of me, I twisted it around my finger where Marcus's engagement ring sat. "I wanted to ask you about the fight Brodie and Marcus had."

She sat up straight, her eyes blazing. "You can't think Brodie killed him!"

"Of course not," I said quickly. "Brodie hardly even knew him. He had no motive to murder him."

Willow bit her lip.

"Tell me what they were fighting about." When it looked like she might not answer, I added, "Please."

"Danny's going to have a fit that I told you. He made me promise not to say anything to anyone, but, seeing as the fight was about you . . ."

"They argued about me? Why?"

She shrugged. "That's what it sounded like to me at least. Marcus was clearly upset."

"He thought Brodie and I . . . He was jealous," I explained.

"Maybe," she said, lifting her slim shoulders again. "He was ranting about losing a Lucky. Brodie stood there, his arms crossed while Marcus unloaded on him. If I didn't know him better, I'd have sworn he was barely paying attention." She hesitated. "I couldn't hear what Brodie said back, but whatever it was, your fiancé lost it. Foolishly, he punched Brodie in the face."

"What did Brodie do?"

Her head moved back and forth. "That's the thing. He didn't do anything. He stood there. I stepped between them a second later." Her eyes lowered sheepishly. "It wasn't the brightest of moves."

"No, it wasn't," I said with a grin.

"I learned just how much when Marcus pulled his fist back to swing again. Brodie grabbed me around the waist with one arm, and then shoved Marcus back with the other. Marcus stumbled back, got tangled in a bar stool, and fell to the floor." She ran her hand down her arm. "A couple of regulars helped him up. He pushed them away, swearing we'd all pay."

I frowned at that.

"And he was half right." She shook her head. "I did end up eating his tab after he stormed off without paying."

Chapter 18

For the rest of the time, we ate in relative silence. The pie sat in my stomach like rotgut. Willow had a few errands to run so she rose to leave. I stood too, shaking off some buttery crumbs from my shirt. Seconds later, the stage whisper of June Wicket, the owner of Wicket Flowers, reached me from the counter where she sat. "I have no idea what a star like him saw in *her*. Brodie Gett panting after her makes more sense. After all, he wants control of Lucky Whiskey."

The awkward teenager inside me burst forth and I wanted to slip away unnoticed. But I wasn't that girl anymore. Holding my head high, I strolled to the door, ignoring June as I gave Cindy Mae a wave. She waved back, the smile on her face growing wider.

Once outside, swamped by humidity and the weight of the burger in my belly, my shoulders slumped. Not from June's assessment. I couldn't care less what she thought. Instead, the daunting task of finding a killer while keeping off the front page of the tabloids and out of jail weighed heavily.

"She's wrong, you know," Willow said from behind me.

As much as I appreciated her coming to my defense, I had asked myself a similar question. Not about Brodie. But about Marcus. For months I hadn't heard a peep from him, and then suddenly he was back in my life, with engagement vengeance. He'd claimed to love me. But I had a feeling there was more to it. Was it intuition or insecurity talking? And more so, what if anything did Marcus's reasons have to do with his murder?

I thanked Willow for meeting me, then headed to Jack's pickup. I considered finding and confronting Evan without Brodie but quickly discarded the idea. For one thing, Brodie had asked nicely for me to wait, and more importantly, Evan was less likely to spit in my face with Brodie there.

I texted Brodie with a plan to confront Evan tonight, using a flurry of emojis. Brodie didn't seem like the emoji type, which made the idea of sending him a random string of them too appealing. The childish behavior made me feel slightly better.

I put my phone back in my pocket and went to tackle the latest leak in our faulty still.

• • •

Rows of large copper stills filled with wash bubbled inside the still room, filling it with the heady scent of the miracle of low wines turning into whiskey. Sweat beaded on my skin, slipping between the valley of my breasts. The heat was unbearable, even though the still I was working on was offline.

Using my tank top, I wiped the preparation from my hands in order to get a tighter grip on the heavy metal wrench that weighed a good five pounds. The valve I was trying to fix, for the fourth time this week, had so far refused to budge, much like the engagement ring on my sweat-soaked finger.

My arms ached from exertion, but I wasn't about to give up. If I was strong enough to run the distillery or even solve a murder, I was strong enough to fix a leaky valve. And if not, I was smart enough to figure out a way to get the job done.

"Need help?" a voice asked from behind me. The sound startled me, and I pitched forward with a squeak, nearly falling into the still. Strong arms grabbed me around the waist, yanking me backward. I landed hard against Brodie, the air whooshing out of his lungs with a harsh hiss.

The ten-foot drop into the empty still probably wouldn't have killed me, but I would've surely busted a leg or two, so my tone wasn't nearly as sharp as it could've been as I asked, "What are you doing here? Spying on the competition?"

He let out a laugh, which turned into a cough. "As if Lucky is any competition."

I spun on him, our faces inches apart. "Really, why are you here? We are supposed to meet up to interrogate Evan tonight, not this afternoon."

Tilting his head, he motioned to the door. "Apparently you haven't looked outside in a while. It's dark out. Has been for a good hour."

"What?" I dropped the wrench on a wooden workbench against the wall and fast-walked toward the exit of the main distillery. Brodie followed behind, though at a more leisurely pace. "What's the rush, Charms? Evan isn't going anywhere."

I shook my head, not bothering to stop. "I didn't make anything for dinner. Jack's bound to be either starving or stuffing his arteries with cholesterol by now."

"Relax," he said. "I brought him a plate of baked trout and sweet potato fries. Not a pat of butter anywhere in the dish, I promise."

I stopped dead. He avoided running into me by an inch. I stared at him for a long moment, rubbing my chin. "You cooked?" Was it possible that Brodie Gett had unplumbed depths? I had my doubts.

He laughed. "Hell, no. Marshall did. I just brought leftovers. I figured you had other things on your mind"—his eyes glittered—"like your meeting with Willow earlier."

"You heard about that."

"Yes, I heard about that." He leaned over me, his breath warm against my heated skin, but not unpleasant. "One of these days you're going to have to start trusting me."

I crossed my arms in an act of self-preservation or defiance. I wasn't too sure which. I blew out a deep breath, admitting what I'd known for a while. "I do. Trust you, that is. About not having killed Marcus at least."

He stepped back, surprise widening his gaze. "Is that so? Then why did you ask Willow about my fight with Savage?"

I lifted my head to meet his gaze. But it wasn't anger I saw in the blue of his eyes. Instead, he looked hurt. Which was ridiculous since someone like me didn't possess the power to hurt a man like Brodie Gett. "You're messing with me." I let out a snort. "I should've known."

Lowering his eyes, he shook his head and stepped by me, never once looking back as he headed for my house. I stood there, staring at his back, wondering if I'd miscalculated.

Chapter 19

An hour later, after eating a good-sized portion of the meal Marshall had prepared for Jack and me, Brodie drove me to Evan's trailer parked at the Wrong Side of the Tracks Trailer & RV Park on the edge of the swamp. *Edge* was probably the wrong word as, technically, the trailer park sat partially in the swamp. Every so often the volunteer firefighters were called out to pull some hapless, sunken residents along with their double-wide from the muck.

Though Evan could've afforded a house that didn't flood every time it rained for the amount of money Jack paid him to be our cooper, he opted for this place. Honestly, I had to admit that, besides my own father, Lucky had never had such a wizard with wood. Evan, for all his other faults, which were many, instinctively understood the oak. When it came to whiskey making, what you put the mother's milk in was as important as what you put in the brew.

Apparently the gift of wood skipped around in the Lucky gene pool too. Much to my dismay. I would've liked nothing better than to rid the distillery of Evan's presence for good. Don't get me wrong, when he actually worked, he did a great job, but all too often I'd find him throwing dice with other employees while on the clock, or skipping work altogether to head up to Atlantic City.

Brodie stopped his Jeep about ten feet from Evan's trailer, which tilted to one side. Other than that, the trailer looked to be in decent shape. The metal had yet to begin to rust, a miracle in Florida, where sun, humidity, and sea air scavenged metals.

Shouts rose from inside the trailer.

I recognized Evan's voice as he yelled, "No! You're killing me!"

Brodie and I shared a quick glance before he jumped from the Jeep. "Stay here, Charms. Do you hear me?"

I nodded but he wasn't paying any attention, his focus on the trailer and whatever mayhem was happening inside. He ran toward the door. I ignored his warning and followed directly after. Rather than blistering me for it, he merely stepped fully in front of me as if trying to protect me. While I appreciated the thought, I wasn't the one needing help at the moment.

Before Brodie could throw the door wide another scream rent the air. This time the sound was loud and filled with such horror that I shoved my palms over my ears. Brodie grabbed the door handle but the knob didn't move. The door was locked from the inside. Without wasting a second he slammed his elbow into the spot just above the handle. The door flew inward with a cry equaling Evan's from only a moment ago.

I followed him through the door, nearly running into his broad back when he stopped. I expected to see bloodshed, and maybe Evan's body on the floor. Instead, I saw dirty clothes, pizza boxes, and beer cans. Everywhere. Evan was, in fact, alive and well, his focus on the MMA fight flickering on his seventy-five-inch TV screen. He screamed at the screen, throwing an empty beer can at it to emphasize his point.

When the round ended, and not a second sooner, he finally turned to us, his eyes widening as if just realizing we were inside the trailer. "Charlotte? What the hell are you doing here? Is it Jack? Is he dead?"

I flinched at the question, grief rising in me at the very idea. But it wasn't the same for Evan. He looked almost happy at the prospect of an inheritance. Not that he had much of one coming. Jack had ensured Lucky would pass to me upon his death. That included the house and all other assets. Evan would receive ten thousand dollars, to be held in trust, until he turned thirty.

And that was all he would get.

Evan didn't know this, of course, which was why he kept pressuring me to sell to Rue.

"Jack's fine," Brodie growled. "We're here for another reason."

Evan's shoulder slumped a little. I wanted to smack him. Brodie must've read my mind, for he reached for my hand, giving it a squeeze. I suspected it was more in an effort to silence me rather than for comfort, though I appreciated it all the same. Now was not the time to lose control. I needed answers from my cousin, not hostility. "Suit yourselves," Evan said, his attention returning to the TV.

Thankfully it was still a commercial break so we hadn't lost him quite yet. "Evan," I began, "I'm sure you know about Marcus's death."

He shrugged. "What's it gotta do with me?"

And that was it. Evan's whole life described in six words. Everything, always, revolved around Evan. He perceived the world in accordance with how every event, no matter how distant or trivial, affected him. As a child he'd displayed the same tendencies. Jack had hoped he'd grow out of it. But it didn't look as if Evan would ever change.

"We're not sure." Brodie lifted a pizza box from the couch and set it on top of a stack of equally grease-coated cardboard on the floor. While I appreciated the leaning tower of Pisa, Evan's leaning tower of pizza didn't hold the same appeal. Not by a long shot.

My stomach lurched at the thought of sitting on the couch. I opted to remain standing when I saw a cockroach the size of a whiskey bottle crawl from one of the boxes. The urge to run screaming from the trailer passed a few seconds later. I took a deep breath through my mouth, not daring to assault my nose with the smell of dirty laundry and moldy pizza.

"Did you kill him?" I asked in a steady voice. I didn't expect Evan to admit to it if he had done the deed, but I had hoped to elicit a reaction.

Instead, he stared at the TV, unmoving.

"Evan," I said, "did you hear me? I asked if you killed Marcus?"

Finally, he turned to me, his eyes blazing. "I'm not the one with motive, Charlotte."

I glanced at Brodie, seeing how he felt about Evan accusing him of the crime. Surprise filled me as Brodie stared back at me, the same questioning look in his gaze. Was Evan referring to me? "Are you suggesting . . . that I killed him?"

"Well, I sure didn't," he barked. "Maybe it was your boyfriend there." He waved to Brodie. Heat rose on my cheeks at the accusation. But Evan wasn't finished. "Maybe Gett didn't like having competition for the distillery."

I didn't dare glance at Brodie, for I'd either see anger or truth in his face. Time for a different tactic, as outright accusing him wasn't getting us anywhere. "Let's assume," I said, "that you didn't have anything to do with Marcus's death."

"Good assumption because I didn't."

For a moment, I really wanted to believe him. While he wasn't the best of relatives, or people for that matter, it would destroy Jack to know that Evan had taken a life. "Fine. But tell me this: before he died, Marcus said he told you *this wouldn't work*. What did he mean by that?"

Evan's face paled a bit but he merely shrugged his shoulders. "Did you ask him?"

I should've. I really should've. But at that moment, I wanted nothing more than to end things between us and get away from the anger in his gaze as fast as possible. "When did the two of you become so chummy?"

"What makes you think that?"

I motioned to the door of the trailer, to the golden-colored car sitting nearby, large rust spots covering its front end. "Because you let him use your Honda. I've never seen anyone else drive it but you."

"So what? We met when I came to see you. It wasn't like I knew him beyond that. He asked for a ride, and I didn't feel like being a chauffeur, so I let him use my car. Big deal."

He was bluffing. The way his right eye twitched gave him away. This was what made him such a poor gambler. Knowing when to hold 'em or fold 'em was all well and good, but a card sharp had to also know how to lie his butt off.

"Fine," I said, nodding my head, "did Marcus happen to mention anyone else in Gett he had problems with?"

Evan lifted his shoulders again.

This was a waste of time. He either didn't know anything or wasn't about to spill his guts to us. Which was far more likely. I glanced to Brodie, who sat on the couch, a frown filling his lips. He caught my eyes, nodding his head as in silent agreement.

"Listen," Brodie said to Evan, "you can either talk to us or to my brother, in a more official capacity. Now, answer Charms's question. Was Savage having issues with anyone else in Gett?"

Evan pushed a shaky hand through his golden hair. "He and Billy James had some words on Saturday night."

"What about?" I drew back. Billy wasn't the type to have words with anyone. At least since he and Sweet Jayme started seeing each other three years ago. She wouldn't put up with that sort of thing. And Billy loved her enough to change his rougher ways.

"Who knows with Billy? Any little thing sets him off."

A recent rumor about Billy banning Evan from the Get-It Saloon flickered through my head. Was Evan tossing Billy's name into the suspect mix as some sort of revenge? I had to talk to Sweet Jayme.

"Anyone else?" I asked. It seemed Marcus wasn't as nearly well liked in Gett as he was in Hollywood. Must've been a real change for a man used to the star treatment. Again, I wondered if there was another reason for his visit to Gett than his asking for my hand in marriage. Though the asking part really hadn't happened.

If Marcus had asked, in that moment, would I have said yes? I told myself no. I hadn't loved him. And, for now, my home was here, in Gett, with my gambling cousin, my grumpy grandfather, and whiskey so fine it made the angels steal more than their fair share.

Evan's eyes flickered back to the TV. A commercial for the Welcome Home Funeral Home popped into view. A somber-looking man spoke in a soothing tone about the inevitability of death, and how it would be a lot easier to plan one's funeral before the event. A shot of an urn laid to rest inside of kayak, which was then pushed out into the Everglades, appeared on-screen.

My skin prickled at the thought of spending an eternity in the swamp. Though it didn't seem to bother the fake family of blue-eyed actors who waved as Grandpa floated off.

The MMA fight came back on.

"Evan?" I prompted.

He remained silent, his focus on the tattooed man in shorts pummeling an equally tattooed one. "We lost him," Brodie said.

I nodded, turning toward the door. The sound of groans and grunts on the TV were echoed by my cousin's own. Apparently watching MMA was almost as exhausting as being a participant.

Stepping into the cool night air, the scent of wet earth and decaying vegetation tickling my senses, I wrapped my arms over my chest. "Let's get you home," Brodie said from next to me, "before Jack has my head for keeping you out past curfew. I hear he keeps his shotgun loaded and ready just in case."

"Not true." I laughed. "I don't let him leave it loaded in the house anymore."

Chapter 20

My plan to stop by Sweet Jayme's house during my morning jog dissolved when I trotted down the stairs. Actually, if I was being honest, it vanished even before I left my bedroom as the scent of fresh coffee, sizzling bacon, and the sound of Sweet Jayme's even sweeter voice reached my senses. The woman could sing almost as well as she cooked, which was saying something. Who could blame Billy James for falling for her?

The thought of Billy brought on a wave of queasiness. I didn't believe for a second he had killed Marcus. But with Evan throwing his name around as a possible suspect, I had to warn Jayme. Plus, Billy might have been the last person, besides the killer, to interact with Marcus.

The scent of food and coffee sent my stomach grumbling with longing as my foot hit the bottom step. Jack was already seated at the kitchen table, a full plate of egg whites and soy bacon on his plate. Every so often, he'd glance up from his meal, glare at Sweet Jayme, and go back to eating. She ignored him, pouring me a cup of coffee and then setting it on the table next to a plate of fluffy scrambled eggs and four slices of thick, brown-sugar-basted bacon.

"Have I told you that you're my favorite person. Ever," I said as I sat in the same chair at the very same table I'd sat in as a child. Jack hadn't changed a thing in the house since I'd left for college ten years before. That made me both happy and sad.

She laughed. "You're way too easy to please."

"If only that was true." I took a sip of the steaming hot chicory coffee in my cup. It tasted sweet and bitter, the perfect combination, followed by a kick of caffeine. I licked my lips as an idea for the next Lucky small batch flickered through my head. Could it be done?

"Did you see the *Gazette* today?" Sweet Jayme asked as she placed the Collier County newspaper in front of me. A picture of myself and Brodie, at his house, was on the front page with the headline *Gett Lucky Involved in Savage Killing*. I snatched the paper up, fearing Jack would see the headline and expire on the spot. Quickly, I tucked the paper under my leg.

"Char girl," Jack growled, "I'm old, not stupid. I've heard what those . . . reporters are saying about you and Brodie Gett. Don't help none when you disappear till all hours of night with that boy."

I winced when Sweet Jayme shot me a knowing grin. "I was home by nine. And nothing is going on between us."

Jack snorted, pushing his empty plate away. He slowly rose to his feet without the use of his cane, which stood against the wall. My heart soared. Jack was on the mend. Soon he'd be back to his old self.

And where would that leave me?

Would I go back to Hollywood? Could I? Not at the moment for sure. The scandal surrounding Marcus's murder would be too much.

"My shows are on," Jack said, disappearing into the living room. The blare of his vintage RCA, but not in the trendy way, TV followed.

Sweet Jayme gave me a smile as she set down her own plate, piled high with eggs and bacon. Though she was rail thin, Jayme could eat as much as a growing boy. We stuffed ourselves in relative silence. Finally, I'd eaten more than enough, and I pushed my plate away, patting my stomach.

Refreshing Jayme's cup of coffee and my own, I asked, "Can we talk?"

She stopped eating mid-bite, setting the fork down. "Okay. Whatever it is, Charlotte, I'm here for you. Always."

Tears burned the back of my eyelids. When I came to live with Jack at the age of five, Sweet Jayme was my closest friend. She kept many of my secrets over the years, and I hers.

When I needed her most, Sweet Jayme took over the task of caretaker and part-time nurse for Jack without hesitation. She loved him as much as I did. "Last night . . . Brodie and I . . ." I began, unsure how to ask whether the love of her life knew anything about a murder.

She leapt up, a wide grin on her lips. "I knew it. Brodie's so good for you." Her gaze fell to the engagement ring still stuck on my finger. "Not to speak ill of the dead, but he is ten time the man Marcus Savage was."

Heat rose on my cheeks until I thought I would explode into a flaming ball of embarrassment. "Oh, God, no, Jayme. Brodie . . . we didn't . . . I would never . . ."

The glow of happiness in her eyes dimmed. "I said something similar three years ago, right before Billy swept me off my feet." At the time, Jayme hadn't wanted a relationship, especially with a roughneck like Billy James. They were from very different worlds, even though they lived in the same town. But he'd worn her down with his kindness and plenty of whiskery kisses.

The nagging guilt in my stomach grew at the mention of her feelings for Billy. "Speaking of Billy . . ." I swallowed hard. "Brodie and I went to see Evan last night. And he . . . Well, he claimed Billy might've been the last person to . . . speak to Marcus on Saturday night."

Her face twisted. "Are you asking me if Billy killed your fiancé?"

"Of course not!"

She relaxed some. "Damn your cousin. He'd like nothing more than to see Billy in jail."

I wiped my mouth with a thin paper napkin. "So Billy didn't argue with Marcus on Saturday night?"

"It wasn't exactly an argument," she said quietly. "Billy took offense to something Marcus did at Jack's party." Her eyes lowered to the table as she traced her finger along the wood. "Billy gave him a warning not to do it again."

"A warning not to do what?"

"It's best if you don't know."

Now I had to know. Curiosity was one of my greatest flaws, or so I'd been told by Jack, Brodie, and a list of cheating ex-boyfriends. Personally, I thought of it as an endearing trait, though one that kept me single, as well as engaged in two murder investigations in the last three months. "Jayme, we've known each other a long time."

"True."

"And in all that time, have I ever done what was best for me?"

She laughed. "Fine. But I don't want you to get upset. I'm sure he didn't mean anything by it."

"*Who* didn't mean *what*?"

Licking her rust-colored lips, she said, "At Jack's party, Marcus asked me back to his motel room." She hurried on when I let out an audible gasp. "It was before you got engaged. I'm so sorry, Charlotte. I didn't want you to find out this way . . ."

A laugh bubbled out of my throat. "I don't believe it."

"I swear it's true."

I held up a hand. Light reflected off the engagement ring. "I'm sure it is. What I meant to say was, I can't believe he propositioned you, and then proposed to me. What a jerk." I twisted the ring, fighting to get it off my finger. The skin under it felt angry and raw, an apt reflection of my feelings for Marcus at the moment. If he wasn't already dead, he'd be in serious danger.

She grabbed my hand, stopping my assault, and then released it. "I'm sure he didn't mean anything by it. He was probably drunk. You know how some people react to good whiskey . . ."

"It doesn't matter," I said, and meant it. "What does matter is, someone killed Marcus, and Billy might become a suspect if Danny finds out. I'm assuming you can alibi him?"

She nodded. "Billy wasn't the one making threats that night."

My eyes shot to hers. "Someone else threatened Marcus?"

"No," she said. "Marcus was the one making threats."

"What did he say?"

"Something about how he'd bankrupt the town, if that's what it took." She shook her head. "No one paid him much mind."

Bankrupt the town? Just how had he planned to accomplish that? "Good." I held my fingers out. "Now, can you help me get this damn ring off?"

"Happy to," she said with a grin. A few seconds later, she held up a bottle of bright blue window cleaner. "This will definitely do the trick."

Chapter 21

An hour later, dressed in a form-fitting emerald sundress with large white flowers dotting the hem, I walked into the Gett Savings & Loan, the princess-cut engagement ring still firmly attached to my finger. Jayme and I had spent much too much time, using every trick we knew, to remove the ring. With no luck.

I was now running late to meet Brodie at the Gett Diner, but securing the loan for our new still took precedence. The old one started making loud groaning noises just this morning. According to Remy Ray, our distiller foreman, in a few days it would stop working altogether.

So I'd either wind up in jail for murder or put Lucky out of business.

Neither option appealed much to me.

I did my best to ignore the diamond, as well as the stares of the bank employees and patrons, as I walked with purpose, if not confidence, to the reception desk. I smiled warmly at Mavis McWillis.

"Can I help you, miss?" she asked, squinting through thick-lensed glasses.

"Good morning, Mrs. McWillis," I said. "I'm so sorry for the bank's loss."

She stared up at me blankly.

"For . . . ah . . . Mr. Moore's death."

"Oh. Right." She nodded. "Such a shame." Her words sounded as hollow as an empty whiskey cask.

I gave an internal wince. "Is there any chance I can talk to the acting bank manager about a small matter?"

"I guess," she said, motioning to a set of uncomfortable-looking plastic chairs next to a desk with a coffeepot on top of it. "Help yourself to some coffee and Mr. Burns will be with you soon."

"Thanks." I walked to where she pointed, debating the wisdom of drinking coffee old enough to date. The choice disappeared as Mr. Burns, a tall thin man with white wisps of hair on his head, said, "Ms. Lucky. What brings you by on such a somber day?"

He was right. I should've waited a few days before approaching the banker about a loan. Jonas Moore's death had to be forefront in their minds and hearts. "I'm so sorry to bother you while you're in mourning," I began.

He drew back. "We all liked Mr. Savage's work, and, of course, are properly shocked by the news of his murder . . ."

"Oh, sorry. I thought you we referring to Mr. Moore."

His face pinched, unpleasantly, as if he'd smelled something foul. "Yes, of course, we are all devastated by his death." His features softened. "As you are by Mr. Savage's, I'm sure."

"Yes, obviously." I stifled a grimace. "Do you mind if we talk privately for a moment?"

"Please." He waved me into his office. Cardboard boxes full of Jonas Moore's treasures sat on the desk. He picked up the boxes, setting them on the floor by his feet, before offering me a seat directly in front of the large, expensive cherrywood desk. He sat too, folding into the chair like a piece of origami. "What can I help you with, Ms. Lucky?"

I leaned forward, explaining about the loan I needed to buy a new still. Mr. Burns listened intently, nodding a few times. When I finished, he wiped his hand over his brow. "We'd need collateral, of course."

"Of course." It certainly wouldn't be the first time we risked the house to support the distillery. If push came to shove, we could sack out in the rackhouse. I filled out the papers detailing the loan, and signed on the dotted line, a sick feeling in the pit of my stomach.

So much was riding on my ability to make good whiskey, up to and including the livelihoods of our thirty employees and the roof over our heads. What if I failed? What if the Lucky whiskey genes had skipped my generation?

Belying my doubts, I held my head high as I left the bank. All eyes were on me and would be until I could find a better suspect in Marcus's murder, one that didn't also have the surname Gett.

• • •

"You have got to be kidding." Danny Gett, dressed in jeans and a button-down shirt, eyed his brother for a long moment. When Brodie didn't laugh, or even smile, Danny groaned. He turned his glare on me. I tried not to squirm under its intensity. "I expected as much from you." He jabbed his finger my way. "But, Brodie, you know better. I can't tell you anything about an ongoing investigation. Especially when my brother is one of the main suspects."

I tilted my head. "One of the main suspects? Who else is one?"

Danny didn't answer.

"Who?" I demanded. "I deserve to know."

He let out a small laugh. "And why is that?"

My mind went blank for a moment. "I was his fiancé."

"And there is your answer." Danny turned back to his brother, ignoring me. I tried not to let his rudeness, along with his words, bother me. But they did just the same. I didn't like his implication one bit, but I kept my mouth shut, for now.

"You know as well as I do that Charms didn't kill Savage. She doesn't have it in her," Brodie said. I nodded, appreciating his confidence in my moral fiber. "She's just not strong enough," he added.

I snorted. What I didn't have in brute force I made up for in brains. If I put my mind to it, I surely could beat a person to death. I winced at the very bizarre morbid thought.

Danny scratched the whiskers on his chin, his gaze on his brother's face before he glanced around the nearly empty parking lot of the Gett Diner. "Hypothetically, it wouldn't take an abundance of strength to pick up a lamp and crack Savage in the head." He turned his stare on me. "Three solid hits to the back of his skull would be all it needed for death to happen within seconds."

My stomach rolled at the image.

"Did you find any physical evidence? The killer's blood? Fingerprints?" Brodie asked, sounding like all the cop shows on TV rolled into one. Many actors, people paid to say lines like that, didn't sound half as convincing.

"Only blood we found, or might've found if this was an *actual* case, was the victim's. We did pull DNA and fingerprints, a whole bunch of them, as you can imagine. Next time I stay at a motel, I'm bathing everything, including myself, in hand sanitizer."

"Oh, gross." I shuddered.

Brodie grinned, and then turned back to his brother. "In *theory*, would anything have been missing? Like, let's say, cash or jewelry?"

With a shrug, Danny said, "If I was guessing, which I am, no money would be found in his wallet, but all twenty-seven credit cards would be accounted for. A pair of diamond cufflinks and a platinum chain would also be located in the nightstand."

"That means robbery is out as a motive," Brodie said. "Damn."

I'd suspected as much. For all his faults, Danny kept the county relatively free of thieves, except for kids occasionally breaking into unlocked pickups.

"You didn't mention his cell phone. Did you find it?" I asked, frowning. Marcus never went anywhere without it, including to bed at night. Ignoring my question, Danny focused on his brother. "Something else to keep in mind, hypothetically, of course."

"Yeah?"

"It looks like he let his killer inside," Danny said. "Just opened the door. Would he have let a man in so easily? Or a virtual stranger?" His gaze shifted my way. "Nope. He had to know his killer, and have a reason to trust they weren't going to murder him."

My hands went to my hips. "Are you implying something, *Sheriff*?"

Brodie waved me off. "Danny's just stating the facts. Isn't that right?"

"If you say so," Danny agreed with a sneer. "Just make sure you watch your back, brother, in case I am indeed implying something."

Chapter 22

Danny drove his patrol car from the parking lot of the Gett Diner, Brodie and I both lost in our own thoughts as we watched him pull away. Mine churned with equal parts anger at Danny's parting shot and fear. Fear that if I didn't find the real killer he'd soon arrest me. Spending my days in an eight-by-ten cell wasn't on my list of vacation destinations. But how would I find the killer without a single lead or better suspect than the man standing next to me?

Apparently Brodie had a similar thought, for as soon as his brother's vehicle exited the lot, he waved me to his Jeep. "We'll go over to the Harker Motel and talk to Wendell. Maybe he knows if Savage had any visitors on the day he died." He hesitated. "Other than you, that is."

The desire to stick my tongue out at him like we were children on the playground was strong. Instead, I straightened my shoulders and gave him my most winsome smile, the one with plenty of teeth.

Brodie snorted. "You do know alligators are known to give a similar grin right before they eat their prey."

Rolling my eyes, I pulled myself into the seat with help from the roll bar. Once I had my seat belt fastened, he started the vehicle and off we went. My cell phone rang as we turned onto Route 29. I reached for the phone while stifling a scream as the Jeep cornered on two wheels.

"Hello," I said once my stomach left my throat.

"Ms. Lucky," Mr. Burns, the banker, said. "I'm glad I reached you. I'm calling about your loan request . . ."

Coldness swept over me even under the bright Florida sunshine. "Is there a problem, Mr. Burns? Did I forget to sign something?"

"The paperwork is in order."

"Good." I blew out a relieved breath.

Mr. Burns stayed silent for a moment. Finally, he cleared his throat, and my heart sank. "Ms. Lucky"—he paused—"it's with great regret that Gett Savings & Loan cannot provide you with a loan."

"What?!" I lowered my voice so Brodie wouldn't overhear. "Please, Mr. Burns, we really need this . . ." I looked to Brodie. His eyes were on me and he slowed the Jeep. I ducked my head so he wouldn't see my face. Luckys didn't beg, at least not with a Gett watching.

"I am sorry, Ms. Lucky."

I slowly pressed End on my phone.

"Was that Sam Burns from the Savings & Loan?" Brodie asked, tearing me from my desperate thoughts. I didn't answer. If I lied, he'd only find out the truth, that the bank obviously didn't have faith in my abilities to run the distillery else they would've signed off on the loan.

Brodie pulled the Jeep to the side of the road and then twisted in his seat. "Charms," he said. I refused to look at him. Instead, I stared at the swampland beyond the metal housing of the vehicle. The marsh swirled with life. With predators and prey. At this moment I felt very much like the latter. "Charms," he tried again. "Look at me."

Taking a deep breath, I did just that. His dark hair looked black under the bright sunlight. I held my hand over my eyes to cut down on the glare. "What?"

"Rue will loan you what you need."

I couldn't contain the scoff that rose in my throat. "Are you kidding me? Rue is the very last person I'd take money from."

He nodded as if he'd expected as much. "What about me? Would you take money from me?"

I was shaking my head before he finished his sentence. Not only would taking money from him be much like taking it from Rue, where would he get the staggering amount I needed? He hadn't worked in over a year, not since his forced retirement from the military. "Thanks," I said with as much graciousness as I could muster. "But I couldn't . . ."

"There is another way."

"What's that?" I pictured myself robbing the Gett Savings & Loan, and a small smile flickered across my lips. At least then Danny would have a real reason to arrest me.

"You could always sell it."

"I will never sell Lucky. Do you hear me?"

He reached for my hand, his fingers warm and firm, as he turned my hand over to show off the two-carat platinum diamond solitaire on my finger. Once again, I'd forgotten all about the engagement ring. "I couldn't . . . It belongs to Marcus's family now . . ."

"Does it? He gave it to you." Brodie tugged on the band. "Why not let it do some good?"

I pulled my hand away, hiding the ring under my other hand. "Do you think Danny really sees me as the prime suspect in Marcus's murder?"

Brodie snorted at the change of subject. "Fine, Charms, have it your way. And yes, I think Danny would like nothing more than to lock you up. Maybe not for Savage's murder, but you've got to admit that since you moved back to Gett, the murder rate has jumped by at least two hundred percent." His shoulders lifted when I shot him a glower. "Maybe more. I never was any good with math."

A lie told with such good ole boy charm, I almost bought it. He sounded so sincere. Almost as much as when he said he had nothing to do with Marcus's death.

Chapter 23

A sense of trepidation filled me as we pulled into the parking lot of the Harker Motel a few minutes later. What if we didn't find a clue to the identity of the real killer inside? Would Danny arrest me? Bile rose in my throat, but I swallowed it down. I refused to give in to the fear. I'd solved one murder. I could solve this one too.

Or die trying.

The ugly thought flickered through my brain.

"Maybe we'll get *lucky*, Charms, and find a new suspect," Brodie said with a smirk.

"I'm so happy that my last name is a source of joy for you," I said sharply, though in truth his joke, while not funny in the least, eased some of my worry. Brodie wasn't going to let me go to jail. For now, we were partners, at least in solving Marcus's murder.

"When we talk to Wendell, let me do the talking," he said.

I rolled my eyes. Chauvinism was a way of life around these parts. For a town with pretty great internet connectivity, in many ways Harker, like Gett, was stuck in the 1950s. Men dealt with men, while women chatted each other up after Sunday service. I'd run into my fair share of boys' clubs in Hollywood, where male directors held way too much power, but the good ole boy network in these parts took chauvinism to new heights. Distributors for Lucky Whiskey asked, time and again, for Jack's opinions even though I'd run the business for the last nine months. "As you wish," I said, bending into a formal curtsy.

"If only you meant it," he said. "Before you get even more bent out of shape, Wendell and I play on the same softball team, so he's more likely to tell me about Savage's stay."

I fell in step behind Brodie as he headed to the motel office, marked with stenciled words declaring it so. A red sign in the window flashed the word *Vacancy*. Not a real surprise considering there were only three cars parked in the lot. Yellow crime scene tape waved menacingly from the balcony.

Brodie opened the door, waving me through. I hesitated on the cusp for a moment, gathering myself. He fingers touched my back, either to propel me forward or to offer comfort. I decided on the former when he added a small shove.

The office was empty, though the scent of acrylic paint fumes and cigar smoke hovered in the air. A silver bell sat on the counter. I touched it softly, resulting in a clang loud enough to crack a shot glass. Brodie winced but didn't comment.

Seconds tickled by, the echo of the bell clapper fading only slightly.

Finally, Wendell wobbled down the hallway toward us, his face a blank canvas, "Oh, hey, Brodie. How long will you and Charlotte be staying?"

If Wendell thought . . . then others might think . . . If Jack heard about this . . .

Brodie's lips curved into a knowing smirk. I jabbed my elbow into his ribs when he didn't clear up Wendell's mistaken impression.

"We are not —" I began.

"It's okay, Charlotte." Wendell gave me a wide, almost tobacco-stained smile. "I'm like Pastor Matt in this regard. No one will know about your . . . time here."

Brodie piped up. "While I appreciate your . . . discretion, Charms and I aren't here to hookup. We have a couple of questions about the night Savage died. Do you mind answering them?"

Wendell shrugged his thin shoulders. "Can't see why not. I told your brother everything I know, but he's the only one. I didn't say boo to that guy with the camera. Especially after he moved rooms because he didn't like the mural I painted in his."

"Wait a minute," I said, glancing around, "the paparazzo is staying here?" Brodie appeared just as concerned by the possibility, for he took two steps to the side. Had he never heard of a wide-angle lens?

"Yeah." Wendell shook his head. "Hasn't let Trish clean in there either."

My forehead wrinkled. "When did he check in?"

Taking out a black notebook, he flipped through a few pages, tracing his finger down the columns with care. "Checked in Wednesday night."

Brodie and I looked at each other.

"Which room is his?" Brodie waved to the rooms facing us, both upper and lower, all with much the same façade. The only thing that stood out was the yellow crime scene tape hanging off the balcony on the side of the building. The exterior paint on the motel was a mixture of tan and gray. Or maybe just faded from the sun. Black iron banisters circled the small enclosed balconies of each room, and a wide front window sat a few inches away from the doorways. Most of the shades, damaged by the sun, were drawn.

Wendell frowned. "I can't tell you that. I took an oath."

I swallowed a smile at how sincere he sounded about his Motelocratic oath. Brodie apparently didn't see the humor in it, for he leaned close to Wendell. "And here I *talked* your daughter's ex out of harassing her after you asked me too." From Brodie's tone, it was clear that talking wasn't the only method of persuasion used.

The older man threw up his hands. "Fine. He's in room three. The one on next to the soda machine."

I turned, focusing on the closed motel room door nearest the vending machine. The shade was pulled tight against prying eyes, or maybe the sun. A maroon-colored rental car with Florida plates sat parked in front. Mud caked its tires and windshield.

"I don't think he's in the room now," Wendell added. "I saw him leave about an hour ago with someone."

Tension eased the coiled muscles in my back. I slumped for a moment until my training kicked in. Actresses always kept their backs straight, heads held high, or so my old acting coach had insisted whenever my shoulders rounded.

"Somebody you recognized?" Brodie asked.

Wendell shook his head.

"What about the night Savage died?" Brodie motioned through the wide front window of the office. "Did you see the guy with the camera or anyone else hanging around?"

Wendell sucked at his teeth. An action as gross as it sounded. "Plenty of people were here on Saturday. We were real busy. Almost all the rooms were booked."

Considering I counted only ten doors, busy was relative. "Did you notice anyone or anything out of the ordinary? Maybe someone hanging around who didn't belong?" Like a villain twirling his mustache menacingly? That was probably too much to ask.

"Can't say for sure." He rubbed his face, leaving a smear of blue paint along his cheek. "Boone was hanging around some."

"Boone Daniels?" Brodie growled. Boone was the scourge of Gett, a drug dealer with a love of guns and assaults. Danny had tried numerous times to lock him up, but, like a palmetto bug, he kept coming back. From personal experience, I knew to stay away from him. "He was here when Savage died?" Brodie's brow narrowed in question.

"No, no. I chased him off before ten." Wendell ran his hand over the counter. "Didn't see no one else."

Damn, Boone would've made a good suspect. "Did you hear anything around the time Marcus died?" Which, according to Danny, had been around three in the morning. "A fight? Screaming? Anything?"

"My hearing ain't what it used to be," he said with a shrug. "You should ask Grace."

"Grace?"

"Grace Moore. Poor dear is staying in the room next door to the scene of the crime." Which explained why she wasn't home when I dropped off Marshall's casserole. Wendell frowned, his eyes growing misty. "I can't imagine losing my Jane. And Grace is so young . . ."

"Thanks. We'll talk to Grace after we get a look inside Savage's room," Brodie said causally.

"Your brother said no one was allowed up there." He waved his index finger at Brodie. "Not until he finished his investigation."

Brodie leaned on the counter, kicking one boot over the other. He appeared completely relaxed to the outside world, though the air around him nearly crackled with energy. "Danny gave us special permission. You can call and ask if you like."

Internally I winced. What was Brodie thinking? If Wendell called Danny, we would likely be arrested for obstruction and tampering before he hung up the phone. The likelihood of both of us winding up in a jail cell before this was all over hovered around ninety percent as it was. Why push it?

Seconds ticked by in silence.

Finally, Wendell shook his head. "Don't make any more of a mess up there."

Brodie straightened, giving his softball teammate a quick nod. "You got it."

Chapter 24

"What would you have said if he decided to call your brother?" I asked as Brodie motioned me up the staircase to Marcus's former room. He followed behind, close enough I could smell the spicy aroma of his aftershave. I tried to place the warm and inviting scent, much like the finest of whiskeys.

"I knew he wouldn't."

"Why not?"

We arrived at the top step. I hesitated on the threshold, afraid of what we might find or worse, what we wouldn't. Talking to Wendell hadn't provided much in the way of a new suspect. And what would happen if we didn't find any clues inside?

Brodie took my arm, turning me away from the doorway to face him. "Why don't you wait here," he said, his face softening with sympathy. "I can look around by myself."

"No." I faced the door once more, but didn't make a move to go inside.

"Danny umps for the league," he said randomly.

I blinked a few times. "What?"

A smirk lifted the corners of his mouth. "Wendell tried to steal second base last season. Danny called him out. Wendell was so mad he spit at my brother, which is when things went from bad to worse for Wendell. Danny tossed him out of the game." He laughed. "Since then, every time those two are together, Danny rubs it in."

My brow crinkled. "What does that have to with anything?"

His laugh deepened. "Wendell has taken to avoiding my brother at all costs. I knew he wouldn't want to talk to him willingly, so I made the offer for him to call Danny." He snapped his fingers. "Worked like a charm" — his eyes found mine — "Charms."

I stifled an eye roll. "I'd say you're an evil genius, but I'd be lying about the last part." The story and our banter eased the tension tightening my body.

"It's a gift," he said with a chuckle, and then quickly sobered as he nodded toward the door. "It's now or never."

Taking a deep breath, I blew it out through my mouth, straightened my back. "Let's do this."

He flipped open a pocketknife he'd pulled from his worn jeans. The blade sparkled in the sunlight. Like butter, the knife sliced through the yellow band of crime scene tape with a bunch of threatening legal language across it.

And just like that, we were in.

Two less-than-criminal masterminds.

Brodie motioned me inside. The room was much like I remembered it, The awful landscape above the bed looking just as bad as it had only forty-eight hours before. Had it really only been two days since I'd stood in front of a very alive and angry Marcus? In too many ways, it felt like a lifetime had passed.

"Looks like someone was searching for something." Brodie waved to the disarray, including an unmade bed and Marcus's designer clothes, which were strewn around. I ran my hand over the shirt Marcus had worn at Jack's party. A shirt that hung over the back of a stained chair.

"In Hollywood, Marcus had a housekeeper."

"So?"

"So he wasn't used to cleaning up after himself."

He snorted.

I started to defend Marcus, but then thought better of it. What could I say? Grown men shouldn't leave their dirty boxers on the floor for someone else to pick up. No matter how much money they had. "Do you see his cell phone? Danny didn't say if he found it."

"I don't see it." He carefully kicked aside Marcus's undergarments to check the floor next to the bed. "This is interesting though."

"What?" I peered over the bed to where he was pointing. Dark bits of plastic sat low in the shag carpet. I came around the bed for a closer look. "Was is that?"

He bent down, picking up a piece. The edges were rounded, but unrecognizable. "No idea."

We continued the search. I opened the closet, finding nothing but expensive apparel. Brodie was busy checking the nightstand by the bed. He picked up the black faux-leather Bible, flipping through the pages. At one particular passage, he froze, his face growing haunted.

"Brodie?" I rushed over. "Are you all right?"

He didn't answer for a long moment. My heart beat faster with each passing second. Something was very wrong. "Please answer me."

He finally did, though it was far from what I expected to hear. "See this white powdery stuff?" He held the Bible out. Crushed between the pages was a small baggy.

My heart dropped into my stomach at his words. "Drugs."

"Yep."

I rubbed my hand over my arm. "Danny didn't mention finding any."

He shrugged. "Maybe that's because he didn't find any. Which means—"

I cut him off. "We finally have another motive for his murder."

Chapter 25

How long had Marcus been using? I thought back to our last meeting, to his flushed face and the sweat on his brow. Had his eyes looked glassy? I should've known or at least asked more questions. I wasn't naïve. In Hollywood, people regularly used and often abused drugs. However, I'd never witnessed Marcus indulging.

Was this why he died? The drug business, from what little I knew, was dangerous. If news reports were to be believed, people were regularly killed for as little as a dime bag of weed.

But here in Gett? It didn't make much sense. Or it wouldn't have, except someone had smashed Marcus in the head with a lamp. My eyes flew to the lamp on the nightstand, or rather to the vacant space where a heavy brass lamp had sat only days before. I let out a groan.

"What?" Brodie tilted his head, and then rushed forward with his hands outstretched. "Charms! Are you all right? You look like you're about to faint."

For a moment, I felt like it too. My head swam and my stomach danced. Bending over, I gulped in a breath and let it out. When that failed to work I repeated the action. Brodie stood by my side looking both uncomfortable and concerned. His concern likely came from the very real fear I would puke on his boots and the crime scene. "Breath. Slow and easy," he said, his hand hovering an inch from my back.

Had I not just realized my fingerprints and DNA were likely all over the lamp, I might've found Brodie's concern humorous. But seeing as Danny's best physical evidence might be my own DNA, I didn't find much to laugh about. "Gee, thanks for the encouragement," I snapped, and then winced. "Sorry."

He shrugged. "Are you feeling better?"

I straightened. When I didn't throw up, I nodded in response.

"What happened? One minute you were fine, and then all the color left your face."

I debated the wisdom of admitting the truth. It wasn't like Brodie could do anything about my fingerprints and DNA on the lamp. And even I had to confess that if the situation was reversed, and it was his DNA on the murder weapon, I'd consider him my top suspect. It was better to keep this revelation to myself, for the moment. Hopefully we'd find Marcus's drug-dealing killer long before Danny arrested me. "I . . . ah . . . Everything is just hitting me all at once." He nodded as if he understood, but his eyes burned with what looked like distrust. A look I instantly took offense to. "If you're done interrogating me, is there anything else you see that we can use to find Marcus's dealer?"

"Only one guy in Gett handles the harder stuff. And you aren't going to like it."

At the same time, with equal expressions of disgust, we said, "Boone Daniels."

• • •

It took some convincing, on Brodie's part, before I conceded that rushing to confront Boone about his drug business and possibly the cold-blooded killing of my accidental fiancé wasn't the smartest of ideas, especially after the last time we'd stopped by his trailer for a similar visit and ended up ducking buckshot.

Instead we decided on a less-violent approach.

Brodie called in an anonymous tip about illegal drug sales to the sheriff's office.

In a matter of hours, Danny would have Boone locked away in a jail cell, unable to shoot at us for simply asking if he had committed a recent murder. "So what now?" I asked as Brodie poked his head from the motel room door to check if the coast was clear for us to leave.

"I'd like to have a chat with that paparazzo," he said, cracking his knuckles with slow, menacing precision. Pop. Pop. Pop.

"You need to brush up on your acting skills."

He laughed. "Too much?"

I nodded.

Shrugging, he motioned for me to exit the room. I paused on the balcony that could only be seen from the small parking lot below. A memory flickered through my head. Marcus, standing at this very rail, a wide smile on his handsome face as the night sky sparkled brighter than the ring he'd mistakenly placed on my finger hours before.

Though it wasn't me he was smiling at.

Like much of our time together, he smiled at the camera instead. A selfie taken for his fans posted on Instagram on the night of Jack's birthday, after the disastrous party. He'd captioned the picture with a clichéd quote, *Shoot for the moon. Even if you miss, you'll land among the stars #blessed.*

I shook off the memory to focus on Brodie, who had stepped from the motel room behind me. "If the paparazzo sees us together . . ."

"I know." He started for the steps. "But he might have some information we need to know, like who told him Savage would be here in the first place. That person could very well be the killer, if this drug angle doesn't pan out."

"I doubt it." I gave him a small smile to soften my words. "I'd bet a bottle of Lucky that it was Marcus, or maybe one of his PR people, who leaked his trip to Gett."

He stopped at the top step, a frown tugging at the corners of his mouth. "Are you serious?"

"Yeah. Happens all the time in LA." I shot him a superior smile. "You don't honestly think actresses jog along the beach in full makeup? Or that big stars just happen to eat at Roscoe's House of Chicken & Waffles on the same night as the paparazzi?" My stomach grumbled. "Though the Obama Special is to die for."

A snort escaped his lips. "You're always thinking about food."

"I spent the last five years on a diet. Yes, I am always thinking about food."

His brow wrinkled. "Why? You look . . . um, slim."

Men. They could never quite describe a woman's body without stuttering like idiots. "The camera adds ten pounds. And too many directors like their actresses half starved."

He shook his head. "So what you're telling me is, you chose to live in a place where people purposely give away their privacy and women don't eat anything but salads, rather than sticking around in Gett."

I guess I had.

He stepped forward, so close to me I could feel the heat radiating from his body. "Charms, I—"

"Oh," a voice said from behind me, "sorry. I didn't mean to interrupt."

I spun toward the woman who'd spoken, nearly knocking Brodie down the stairs in the process. He recovered quickly, placing his hand on my back to steady us both. My cheeks heated. "You aren't interrupting. We were just . . ."

"Grace," Brodie said pointedly. "How are you holding up?"

The widow gave us a watery smile. "It's so hard. Everything reminds me of Jonas."

The truth of her words was written on her face. Her eyes were red-rimmed, as if she'd cried herself to sleep. She wore no makeup and her hair looked unkempt. A complete reversal from the woman I'd met a few days before. Gone was the sparkle, the spark, in her eyes.

"I couldn't stand to stay at our house without him," she said as she swiped a tear off her cheek. She wobbled on her feet, and for a second I worried she'd collapse. I reached out to steady her. The scent of alcohol clung to her. "Are you on your way somewhere?" I motioned to the parking lot and a bright red BMW below. The kind of car one expected a banker's wife to drive.

She nodded, again staggering. "I need to talk with Pastor Matt about the service. Jonas deserves the best."

"Why don't you let me drive you?" I said. No way was I allowing Grace to get behind the wheel. Not in her current condition. Grief and alcohol often mixed way too well.

She frowned, as if confused by my offer.

Not wanting to hurt her feelings, I said, "I need to speak with the pastor too."

"Why . . . Oh, yes, about the death of your fiancé." She grabbed my arm, her nails digging into my skin. "I was so sorry to hear about his passing. You must be devastated." A hiccup escaped her lips. "Jonas and I knew our time together was short, but to lose the man you love right after you get engaged . . ."

Brodie released a quiet snort. Luckily Grace wasn't paying him any attention. Her eyes were on mine, filling with sympatric tears. Sympathy I didn't want, nor deserve. "Brodie," I said and turned to him, "I'm going to drive Grace to the church, and then walk home. We should catch up later to . . ." I let my voice trail off, hoping he'd understand. We still needed to talk to Boone, and the paparazzo.

"Right," he said. "I'll hang out a bit, see if I can have a chat with our *friend* in room three."

I took Grace's hand, helping her down the steep stairs and into the passenger seat of her car. I moved to the driver's side, pausing before joining her. My eyes scanned the rooms above.

Both looked so similar, the only difference being a single black unit number on the door. Could Marcus's death be as tragic as a wrong room number?

Brodie raised an eyebrow. "What are you thinking?"

I shook my head. "Nothing. Text me if you find out anything useful from our *friend*."

"Will do," he said. "Better ask Grace if she heard anything that night before she tears up again."

"Will do," I echoed.

And with that, I dropped into the sleek leather seats of Grace's BMW.

Chapter 26

"I hope I didn't ruin your . . . conversation with Brodie Gett," Grace said as we drove along Route 29 toward Gett, Harker and the crime scene in the rearview mirror. My mind swirled with possible suspects. Too many suspects if Brodie was right and someone outside Gett had used Marcus's visit here as an opportunity to commit murder.

"Uh-huh," I murmured.

"The two of you are close?"

I snapped back to the conversation at hand. Was she implying something? "What?"

"You and Brodie, you're friends?"

"Yeah. Friends." I added, "Just friends."

"I wasn't suggesting . . ."

"Sorry," I said. "Since Marcus's murder, the tabloids are saying the worst things about us."

"I know how that feels." When I looked at her in question, she held up a hand. "Maybe not exactly. But people around here made all sorts of terrible assumptions about Jonas and me when I first came to town. It hurt, but mostly I felt sorry for the wonderful man I'd married. His own employees were gossiping behind his back like those old ladies at the Curl & Dye."

From how the bank employees had reacted to his death, her wonderful husband hadn't been all that wonderful. But I respected her desire to whitewash the man she loved. "I'm sorry for your pain."

"Thank you."

"Do you mind if I ask you about Saturday night?"

"Of course not," she said. "I already told Danny everything I know, but I'm happy to repeat it."

"I appreciate it," I said, tapping my hand on the buttery soft leather on the steering wheel. "Do you remember seeing or hearing anything unusual?"

"In all honesty, I don't remember much." A single tear formed in her eyes and then rolled down her cheek. I quickly looked back at the road. She said, "I was having trouble . . . sleeping, so I took two Xanax, and went to bed around eleven."

My heart sank.

"Though something woke me around three in the morning. It could've been a fight, but I couldn't say for sure."

Damn Danny for not mentioning Grace or her statement. Just like a Gett to keep the information I needed to himself. "Anything else that you remember? Any little thing can help."

She hesitated. "I remember that I got out of bed and looked out the window. It was very dark, and I could barely make out the cars below. I think I saw someone get into a car, but again, I couldn't swear to it."

Excitement built within me. "What kind of car?"

"I'm really bad with brands." She blew out a harsh breath. "Jonas knew all about cars. He bought this one for me right after we were married."

"Do you remember if the car was a two-door or a four? What color was it?"

Silence filled the car. I looked over to make sure she hadn't passed out. Luck was on my side, for once, for her eyes were wide open. "Gold. The car was gold. A two-door. Or maybe four." She ran a hand over her face. "Rusty too."

Bile rolled up my throat. "The car had rust spots? Where?"

"On the hood," she said. "Sorry. That's all I remember."

"Had you seen the car before? Maybe parked in the lot earlier?"

"I can't say for sure."

I swallowed, hard. "Okay."

"Is it important?"

Very much so, but I didn't want to tell her so. If she was right, someone, likely my own cousin, had driven off right after Marcus's murder.

Chapter 27

I pulled into the dirt lot of the small church with care. Pastor Matt opened the door and gave us a wave, a look of surprise on his face as I emerged from the driver's seat. "Charlotte? I was expecting Mrs. Moore."

"I drove her," I said. "She's feeling a bit . . . under the weather."

The woman in question staggered out of the car, holding the door for support. The pastor frowned, moving forward to help her. She waved him off, turning to me. "Charlotte wanted to discuss funeral arrangements for her fiancé."

His head shot up. "Is that so?"

"I . . . ah . . . Yes."

A kind smile crossed his rather plain face, giving it depth. I could see why all the marriage minded mommas had their eyes on him. "Please, come inside." He waved to Grace and then myself. "Both of you, and we can make the proper arrangements for both men."

Reluctantly, I followed the pastor and Grace into the church. What had I gotten myself into?

"My office is toward the back," he said.

Incense tickled my nostrils as we crossed the threshold, and I had to stifle a sneeze. I hated that smell. It reminded me of death. Of waiting for my parents to come home, when they never would. Of watching the beep of the heart monitor in Jack's hospital room.

"Excuse me for a moment." Grace's face grew greenish. "I need to . . . freshen up."

Before either of us could speak, she put a hand over her mouth and ran for the small bathroom marked with the outline of a 1950s housewife. I started to follow, but the pastor stopped me with his next words. "I am so very sorry for your loss."

"Thank you." I looked toward the bathroom door. "Maybe I should . . ."

"Give her a moment." He shook his head with reverence. "Jonas's death has been especially hard for her."

"I know the feeling." Thinking of the moments when I wasn't sure if Jack would live. The pain. The fear. The words left unspoken between us.

Unfortunately, the pastor misunderstood my words. "It helps to talk about it. About him. How did you and Marcus meet?" Once again, he motioned me forward, down a long hallway with dark paneling. I looked to the door where Grace had disappeared, debating. The harsh sounds of retching made up my mind.

"We met on the set of *War Dogs*." I didn't mention the fact I was working the craft services table at the time. My career hadn't quite taken off as I'd hoped and I had to pay rent somehow. Unlike most stars, Marcus hadn't avoided eye contact with the little people serving him snacks. Instead he'd given me a sparkling smile, and we started to chat.

"Please, have a seat." Pastor Matt motioned to the chair in front of a plain, unencumbered desk once we entered his small but cozy office. The room suited him. Not fancy or flashy, but steady. Dark wood paneling filled the room, as it had the hallway, making the interior dimmer than need be. Then again, maybe the obscurity helped people spill their sins. Books lined the shelves looking well-read and loved. A tree of sort, with large nuts straining its branches, sat in the corner, under the filtered light coming through the stained-glass window.

"What sort of service are you thinking about?" the pastor asked, taking a seat opposite me. He folded his hands into a steeple.

A wrinkle formed on my brow. "Service?"

A lone, sandy-colored eyebrow rose. "For your fiancé."

"Oh. Right," I said, licking my dry lips. Was lying to a pastor a sin? I couldn't quite remember if it was a sin with a capital *S* or more of a lesser one, punishable by cleaning chalkboards after Sunday school. Why risk it. "Forgive me, Pastor, but I'm not really here to make arrangements for Marcus."

"Is that so?"

I nodded. "I ran into Grace, and she . . . wasn't in any condition to drive over here, so I offered."

"I see." He ran a hand along his cheek. "Will Mr. Savage's family be handling arrangements then?"

"I . . . ah . . . I'm not sure." I hesitated. "I don't really know them."

"I'd be happy to be in contact with them to make arrangements once the police release . . . his remains," he said, uncapping the pen on his desk. "Are his parents still living?"

I shook my head. "I don't think so. He has a sister, but I don't think they are close."

He smiled kindly. "It's my belief that every man, women or child should be given a proper send-off. Why don't we hold a small memorial service for him on Sunday following mass?" He paused, his gaze lowering to the desktop. "It won't cost anything, and it . . . might help clear up a few misconceptions about your relationship."

"I don't understand."

His face flushed red. "If people see your grief . . . it might end those unfortunate rumors . . ."

"I see." While I didn't like using Marcus's eternal rest this way, the pastor did have a point. "Let me think about it."

"Of course." He nodded once. "In case you decide to go ahead with the service, let me ask a few questions about Mr. Savage, get a feel for the man beyond his fame. Did he have any pets? Maybe a favorite childhood one?"

The bizarre question caught me off guard. "I don't see . . ."

"I know it's odd, but mourners enjoy a funny pet story. Makes the deceased feel more alive somehow. But we can skip that question for now if you'd prefer."

I nodded.

"Did Marcus have a favorite book? Maybe a movie he watched again and again?" He paused, continuing when I had no answer. "Did he support any charities? Was he a religious man? Spiritual?"

"We didn't . . . I'm sorry, I don't know."

He reached for my hand, patting it. "It's okay, Charlotte. People who've been married for years often don't know what their significant other is up to most of the time."

"That's true of some couple," Grace said as she walked into the office, steadier on her feet. "But not with Jonas and me." She looked unsure for a moment. "Isn't that right, Pastor?"

"I'm sure it is," he said.

"Thank you, Pastor, for your help. I'm meeting Jack for lunch in a few minutes so I must be going," I lied, without blinking an eye. Why not. My soul was likely damned already for misleading him in the first place. "I'll leave you and Grace to your meeting." He started to rise, but I waved him off. "I'll see myself out."

"I'm here if you need anything," he said.

Grace gave me a wan smile as I closed the door behind me. I blew out a long breath as the weight of what little I'd known about Marcus made my shoulders sag.

Chapter 28

On my walk from the church to the Lucky family home, a patrol car drove slowly by me, and then stopped a few yards ahead. For a few seconds the desire to run as fast as my legs could carry me in the other direction filled me. Instead, I held my head high as I moved toward the car. If I was to be arrested for murder, I'd do so with every ounce of Lucky grace.

Before I reached it, Danny Gett uncurled his long frame from the vehicle. I wasn't too surprised to see him. Not with the way my luck normally went. "Sheriff," I said as sweetly as I could muster. The effort cost me. But seeing as I'd recently disturbed his crime scene, albeit without his knowledge, I owed him that much.

"Ms. Lucky," he said with a nod. "You haven't seen my brother recently?"

I shook my head with affected sincerity. "Not since our conversation with you this morning."

"Is that so?"

Rather than answer, I asked, "Why? Did something happen?"

"You could say that." His eyes burned into mine. "I received a report about an assault at the Harker Motel."

"Assault?" I swallowed hard. Was Brodie hurt?

"Yes. Assault." He motioned up the road. "I was on my way to the scene when I happened by you."

"And you thought to check on me. How sweet."

He rolled his eyes. "If I find out that you or my idiot brother are involved in this, you're going to find out how not so sweet I can be. Do you understand me?"

I nodded.

With a growl, he stuffed himself back in the car, flipped on the overhead blue and red lights, and sped off, leaving a trail of gravel and questions in his wake. I pulled my phone from my pocket and quickly dialed Brodie's number.

"Yeah," he said in lieu of the more formal hello. The single word had never sounded so good to my ears. He was all right.

"Are you still at the motel?"

"Yeah."

"Your brother is on his way there now." I hesitated. "Please tell me you didn't hurt the paparazzo."

Silence.

My heartbeat increased. "Oh, Brodie."

"It wasn't me, Charms. I found him in the alley behind the motel, unconscious. Someone knocked him around pretty good but Lester thinks he'll survive."

Relief made my knees weak, and then Brodie's words finally penetrated. "Do you think it was the same person who killed Marcus?"

I could practically hear his shrug through the phone. "Don't know. I'm going to drive up to the hospital, see if he's alert and if he can answer a few questions before Danny gets there."

"Okay. Call me if . . ."

"I will."

We hung up, and I walked the rest of the way home. I kept looking back over my shoulder, unable to shake the feeling that the killer was waiting, watching from the shadows.

• • •

Before I went into the house, I decided to check the recently repaired still. If it was too hot, an entire batch of wash could be ruined. Same was true if it was too cold. Whiskey was almost as temperamental as the maker. I meant Jack, not myself. I was as easygoing as they came.

Luck was on my Lucky side, for the still was heated to the perfect 185 degrees. In a few hours, we'd distill the wash again. At Lucky, like our forefather in Ireland, we distilled our whiskey three times. One more for luck, Jack liked to say.

All around me the distillery bustled with longtime workers. People who were more family than employees. Generations of people worked at Lucky Whiskey, proud of what we accomplished. But for how long? Without a new still, Lucky Whiskey wouldn't get to the market on time, and chances are we would be in direr straits in the next year. I didn't know where to turn or what to do. Not yet at least. I vowed to find a way to keep the distillery running until my last breath.

I owed Jack as much.

Remy Ray stopped me as I turned to leave the still room. "Hey there, girl," he said.

I winced but didn't comment on his calling me girl. Nothing I said would dissuade him from using the term. Even after the company meeting on harassment less than a month ago. Add in the fact Remy used to change my diapers, and any leverage I had flew out the window. "Hi, Remy Ray. Anything to report?"

A wide smile cracked his wrinkled face. "The Best boys are at it again."

"How bad is it?"

"Derrick cracked a bottle over Adam's head. Seems they are both trying to catch the eye of that Drift girl."

I winced. "Is Adam all right?"

"Of course. You know that boy's head is made of concrete." Remy laughed.

"Well, that's good." I wiped sweat from my forehead. "Dock Derrick the cost of the bottle, and warn him that if it happens again, I'll be forced to take care of it."

"That's enough to scare anyone straight."

I frowned. "What's that supposed to mean?"

Remy Ray flushed, twin spots of red filling his cheeks. "Well, girl, most people around here, not me though, think you killed your man."

"What?!"

He gave me a small smile. "Don't worry none."

"How am I not to worry? The town already believes I'm a vandal, and now they blame me for a murder."

His shoulders lifted with a shrug. "Girl, ain't nobody blaming you."

"But you just said . . ."

He snorted. "I know what I said. I ain't that old." His stark white hair and wrinkled face suggested otherwise, but I wasn't about to add abusing his feelings to the list of my wrongdoings. "What I meant is, no one blames you for killing a man in need of killing."

"But I didn't kill him!"

He patted my arm. "'Course you didn't. That ain't your way."

"Thank y—"

He shook his grizzled head. "If you wanted the man dead, you'd have done it with more finesse. Probably poison or some such thing."

I threw up my hands and charged out of the still room.

Remy's chuckle followed in my wake.

Chapter 29

With more force than necessary, I stormed to the Lucky family home. The front door was open, but I didn't see Jack anywhere inside. His inability to remember to lock the door was an ongoing argument. He claimed no one in Gett locked their doors. Which might've been true, but that didn't mean we shouldn't. Especially now, with a killer on the loose.

"Jack?"

Eerie silence descended. The kind of silence that didn't fit. Blood pounded in my ears as I strained to hear the slightest creak of the house settling, or better yet, Jack's gruff voice. Where was he? My mind filled with all sorts of scenarios, each more horrifying than the one before. Maybe Jack had another heart attack? Was he lying hurt somewhere?

Before my imagination got the best of me, a sheet of paper on the table by the door caught my eye. I picked it up, scanning the words with relief. Jack was fine. He'd gone off, to do some stuff, *that was none of my business.*

I headed for the kitchen for a Diet Coke. I never made it. A loud thud overhead stopped me in my tracks. Squirrels in the attic, I decided when silence descended once again. Jack was always complaining about the terribly cute vermin.

In the kitchen, I started my quest for food in the cabinet closest to the oven. The secret place where Jayme hid anything outside Jack's doctor-ordered diet. Things like chips and full-fat cookies. Either option sounded good at the moment. The blue and white of a potato chip bag put a smile on my face as my fingers curled around it.

The first chip was as good as the next. I ate half the bag before I knew it. Disgust warred with fat-fueled satisfaction. Satisfaction won out. I lowered myself to the couch, kicking my feet up on the coffee table in front of me. I closed my eyes and recounted what I'd learned so far.

Marcus was involved, somehow, in drugs. Which made sense as to why Wendell saw Boone Daniels earlier that night. He probably sold Marcus the drugs. Did that mean Boone also killed him because of it?

Additionally, Grace saw Evan's car speed from the motel around the time of Marcus's murder.

Another noise caught my attention. It was a scraping sound, like someone moving something heavy. Someone else was in the house. "Jayme?" I called out, hoping to hear her sweet, singsong voice respond.

Footsteps pounded overhead. I ran for the stairs. As I reached the top, I paused, listening again. Had the noise come from Jack's bedroom? The one he'd slept in up until his heart attack. Or was the sound closer to my own bedroom?

Before I decided, a figure all in black ran straight for me, arms raised.

I let out a scream loud enough to shatter every whiskey bottle in Gett. A body slammed into mine. The air left my lungs in a whoosh as we vied for position on the steps. My scream cut out mid-bellow, my arms flailing.

Off balance, I started to fall backward, down the steps. My elbow slammed into the wall, and I let out another yell, this time filled with pain. Desperately, I scrambled for the banister, for anything really. Anything to save myself from crashing down the rest of the wooden steps and breaking my neck like a damsel in a Victorian novel.

Luck was on my side, barely. I managed to grip the railing, my shoulder wrenching in the socket. More pain jerked up my arm, bringing tears to my eyes. The front door slammed as the person who pushed me down the stairs made their escape.

Breathing hard, I sat up, accessing. My elbow hurt, and the bare parts of my skin on my arms and legs were scraped raw. Otherwise, nothing seemed broken. I would live, I decided. That was, once my heartbeat slowed to a normal rhythm. I took steady, even breaths until my legs felt able to hold my weight. Slowly I stood, holding the banister for extra protection. Better safe than sorrier.

I climbed back up the stairs to see what, if anything, was stolen by my assailant. I checked Jack's room first. My grandmother Jennie's jewelry box, filled with family heirlooms, sat on the dresser next to a pair of gold cuff links Jack used on special occasions.

I headed for my bedroom next. The door was open. I remembered shutting it before I left. With the tip of my shoe, I pushed the door wide, stifling a gasp when I caught sight of the mess surrounding me. Books, papers, and clothes were scatted everywhere. The thief had emptied every drawer in their search. Bits of glass crunched underfoot as I walked deeper into the mess.

On the floor next to my bed laid my iPad, the screen shattered beyond repair. I pulled the drawer of my nightstand open, and shook with relief as my mother's wedding ring sat where I'd left it, folded in a piece of red cloth, over eighteen years ago.

I pulled my phone from my pocket, dialing the only number I could think to call at the moment. Brodie answered on the second ring. "Hey, Charms, what's up?"

"Someone broke into the house," I said, surprised at how shaky my voice sounded.

"Are you hurt?"

"No." I glanced down at the blood now dripping from the cut on my elbow. "Not really."

"Wait outside. I'll be there in fifteen minutes. Do you hear me?"

I frowned, an edge of steel entering my tone. "Of course I hear you. You're yelling."

"I'm on my way."

Though his words were growled, relief so great my knees grew weak filled me. Which annoyed me to no end. I didn't need Brodie Gett to rescue me. I was a strong, independent woman. I straightened to my full five-six and walked confidently to the stairs. Where I stood, frozen, replaying my near-death experience.

That's where Brodie found me fifteen minutes later.

This time with a small, albeit grim smile on my face.

Chapter 30

"Charms? Are you all right?" Brodie asked, his voice low and calm, like he was talking to a small child. "Talk to me, sweetheart."

His tone set me on edge instantly. "I am not your sweetheart."

"That's my girl." He laughed at my heated glare. "So what . . . You're bleeding." All humor left his face as he rushed up the stairs, grabbing my arm with surprising gentleness. He turned my wrist until my elbow faced him.

I tried to pull away, but he held fast. "I'm fine. Really. It's a scratch. It stopped bleeding ten minutes ago."

While a glower still filled his face, he nodded once and released my arm. He stared at the wall where my body had scrapped away the paint as I fell. "You could've broken your neck."

Not a thought I relished. "They were looking for something."

"What?" His eyes widened. "Are you saying this was more than a robbery?"

"Burglary," I corrected.

"What?"

"A robbery is when you take something from a person, a burglary is when you steal from a place."

A burst of laughter flew from his lips. "As long as I live, Charms, I will never understand the way your mind works."

I tried not to take offense, but a part of me felt a sharp stab of rejection. I would always be the nerdy girl at odds with the more popular football quarterback. I shook off the feeling, my tone sharper than intended when I responded, "At least I have a mind."

"Ouch." He staggered back as if wounded. I grabbed his arm, yanking him toward me and away from the top step. "Be careful, you idiot."

"I didn't know you cared."

I snorted. "I just don't want you to wreck more of my wall with your overgrown body."

"Point taken," he said. "Now, back to my original question. What makes you think this wasn't just some interrupted . . . burglary?"

I ran my hand over my battered arm. "Because I don't have anything worth stealing. Not really."

"What can you remember about your attacker?"

I shrugged. "It happened so fast . . . I'm not sure I even got a good look at him."

"So it was a man. That's a start. What else?"

I shook my head. "Honestly, I'm not sure it was a guy. It could've been a woman. Whoever it was, I don't think they wanted to hurt me."

Brodie snorted. "And yet, here you are, caked in dried blood."

Since I'd first called him, I had racked my brain to figure out what the person wanted. Was it somehow connected to Marcus's murder? If so, how?

"Charms?" he asked when I didn't respond. "Are you sure you didn't smack your head?"

To prove to him that I was fine, I headed down the stairs.

Brodie followed, pausing at the place in the wall where my elbow had hit. He stood there, frowning at the scrapped paint for a long minute. "I don't like this. It's getting too dangerous. First the cameraman and now you."

"I—" The whoop of a siren cut my words off as red and blue flashing lights refracted off the windows. "Did you call your brother about the break-in?"

"No." Brodie headed to the front door. I followed behind, fear filling me. Was Danny about to arrest me for Marcus's murder? I pressed my hand to my rolling stomach. Brodie opened the door.

"I need you to come to the station to answer some questions," Danny said. It wasn't a request. With deep breath, I stepped forward, hoping Danny would forgo the handcuffs. The rumor mill would be swirling enough with news of my arrest.

"Not you," he barked. "Brodie Gett"—he hesitated, voice strained—"you are under arrest for the murder of Marcus Savage."

Chapter 31

"This is crazy," Brodie said to his brother. "You damn well know I didn't have anything to do with his murder."

"Do I?" Danny snapped. "Then explain how it is a surveillance camera across the street from the Harker Motel caught you, literally, running from the scene?"

My head snapped up. "What?"

Brodie blew out a harsh breath. "I didn't kill him, Charms. I swear it."

"I suggest you remain silent," his brother said. "Now." Taking Brodie by the arm, Danny yanked him toward the waiting police car and pushed him into the back. I struggled to gather air into my lungs as Danny's words penetrated my mind. What had Brodie been doing at the motel? Had he lied to me from the beginning? My gaze locked on Brodie's through the back window of the patrol car. And in my heart, I knew Danny had it wrong. But just how wrong?

I needed to see that surveillance footage.

I pulled my phone from my pocket and dialed.

• • •

"How could you arrest your own brother, Daniel Gett?" Rue Gett waved her cane at her grandson, her face and voice ridged with fury. I almost felt sorry for Danny.

Almost.

"Now, Rue," he began, only to be cut off by a smack to his shin with the wooden cane. He cursed, which resulted in another thwack. "I have a job to do. I can't just ignore evidence."

She frowned at him. "I expected better of you."

"Brodie's on tape, running from the scene."

"I'm sure there is a perfectly good reason for it." She nodded when Danny stared at her like she'd grown an extra head. "Have you asked your brother?"

He snorted. "I was about to when you and the *unlucky* cavalierly rushed in."

She raised the cane again, but he sidestepped. "I want to see this surveillance footage. Now."

108

The way she bellowed her order, I expected Danny to jump to attention, as I'd done. Instead, he shrugged. "I can't show it to you."

"Is that so?" she asked with icicles dripping from each word.

"Yes. I'm sorry. But you have to understand. This is a homicide case, not some jaywalking ticket you can talk Brodie's way out of." He paused. "Best thing you can do, either of you, is to hire him a lawyer and mind your business."

Rue glowered at her grandson, but he refused to budge. She grabbed my arm, ushering me from the sheriff's office. We stood on the sidewalk outside, the afternoon sun beating down on us. "We'll see about that," Rue said.

"What do you plan to do?"

Rather than answer my question, she said, "I need a phone."

I quickly handed her mine. Her bony fingers flew over the keyboard like a teenager as she dialed a number. "Let me speak to Bert," she said when someone answered the call. "Yes, tell him it's Rue Gett."

Not more than thirty seconds passed when Bert came on the line.

"Yes, Bert, you can help me," she said. "Call my grandson, and demand he allow me access to some security footage." She paused to listen while Bert spoke. "I'll give you two minutes." She angrily disconnected a few seconds later.

"Set a timer, Charlotte," she ordered me. I did so without question or hesitation. My shins had taken enough abuse for one day.

One minute and seven seconds later, Danny came charging out of the sheriff's office. He skidded to a stop when he saw us. "You tattled on me to the county commissioner? You do know Bert isn't my boss. That I'm elected by the people of Collier County."

She shrugged daintily. "True, but Bert can cut your budget, and then you won't be able to afford all those fancy toys you want in order to protect and serve."

His face reddened. "By fancy toys, I'm assuming you mean new patrol cars?"

Had I not wanted to see the surveillance footage so badly, I might've felt genuinely sorry for Danny. Being Rue Gett's grandson as well as the sheriff had to be hard.

"Let us see the footage and we won't bother you again. I

promise," I said quietly as the two of them shot daggers at each other.

"Fine. But don't try and manipulate me again." He glared at Rue and then me. "Either of you."

A few minutes later, seated in the conference room, gray walls all around us, Danny pressed Play on a laptop. A grainy black-and-white image of a parking lot across from the motel appeared on-screen. If I remembered correctly, the lot belonged to the Harker Bass & Go Shop. Why a bait shop needed external surveillance cameras was beyond me. Was there a string of bass-related crimes that I didn't know about? I honestly hoped so.

The screen flickered a few times as the time stamp on the bottom of the image counted off minute after minute. Around three in the morning, Danny pointed at the figure jogging through the bottom of the shot. "There's Brodie. Right around the time the ME said that Savage died."

"I don't believe it," Rue said, though her voice wavered. "Brodie is no killer."

Danny nodded, his voice low when he spoke. "Not the Brodie who left us to join the Army, but the one who came home a year ago? Can you honestly say the same?" He paused, his face grim. "I don't want it to be true either. But the proof is right there."

Rue stood, her hand shaking on the head of her cane. "Talk to your brother before you do anything. Ask him."

Danny silently nodded, following Rue out of the room. I sat, staring at the screen. Danny was wrong. Maybe not about his brother being at the scene, but that didn't make Brodie a killer. I pressed Play on the laptop once again. A few minutes after Brodie passed the camera, a pair of headlights cut through the darkness, flaring like rockets on the night vision lens. I squirmed, half terrified to see Evan's Honda. My terror soon turned to annoyance as the lens flare faded without the car coming into view.

I stood, my eyes still on the now-frozen image of the vehicle's headlights. Danny charged into the conference room, his eyes burning. "Are you happy now? Rue didn't need to see that, but you couldn't leave it alone."

Guilt tickled the back of my throat. He wasn't wrong. I felt bad for upsetting Rue, but it was for a good cause. "Did you watch the rest of the footage, Danny?"

If his gaze could actually start fires, I'd go up faster than whiskey-soaked kindling. "It's *Sheriff*. And of course I watched it. Do you think this is my first day on the job?"

"So you saw the headlight?"

"Yes. And your point?"

I thought it was obvious, but if he wanted me to spell it out, I would. "That could very well be the killer pulling out of the motel's lot."

"Or Dennis Fox making his morning milk deliveries." He snorted. "Quit playing detective, and focus on keeping Lucky afloat."

"I wouldn't have to play at anything if you'd do your job," I muttered under my breath.

"What'd you say?"

"Not a thing," I said with a smile. "Do you mind if I have a chat with one of your prisoners?"

He crossed his arms. "I'm not letting you talk to Brodie until after I do."

"Not a problem." I nodded. "I want to speak to Boone Daniels."

Chapter 32

Danny begrudgingly sat me down in an interrogation room while a deputy went to get Boone. "What's this all about, Charlotte?" Danny asked.

I licked my lips, unsure how much to tell him. I decided to ask a question first. "Did the medical examiner do a tox screen on Marcus?" Long nights reading over police drama scripts had finally paid off. Though not in the way I'd suspected a year ago.

He gave an obnoxious snort that bounced around the cement walls. "No cop talks like that."

"Just tell me, did Marcus have any drugs in his system?"

"Why? Was he a regular user?"

I gripped my hands together to keep from choking Danny. "I'll tell you why I ask, if you'll tell me the truth about any drugs. Deal?"

For a few seconds I thought he'd refuse, but he finally held his hand out. "Deal."

I took the offered appendage, shaking it. "You first."

He laughed. "I will never understand what Brodie sees in you."

I didn't respond.

"The ME didn't find any drugs in his system." He paused. "Happy?"

"You're kidding."

"Do I look like I'm the sort of man who kids, as you put it?"

I blew out a breath. "Not really." But how was that possible? Brodie and I had found drugs in the motel room. Why else would Marcus have drugs in his room unless he was using them?

His gaze lowered to mine. "You really didn't know him well."

"No, I didn't."

"Let's be clear." His moth thinned. "From this moment on, you are done investigating this murder. If I hear different, I will lock you away for obstruction."

"But—"

"The penalty for which is up to three years in jail." He stopped, his eyes hard. "How would Lucky, or more importantly, your grandfather survive without you for that long?"

Before I could respond, in a way that probably wouldn't help my plight, a deputy knocked on the door. Seconds later, Boone entered, a leer on his lips and handcuffs around his wrists. "Well, well, ain't I lucky," he said with a laugh, as if I hadn't heard that one a hundred times before.

Danny shoved Boone into a metal chair across from me, locking the handcuffs to the steel hook welded to the table. "Behave yourself," he warned. I didn't appreciate the fact he looked to both Boone and me when he said it. "A deputy will be outside. And Charlotte," he said, "remember what I said. Three years."

With that Danny disappeared through the door, leaving me alone, very alone at that, with Boone. I tried to conceal the rush of revulsion skirting my skin. He gave me a tobacco-stained smile, all rotting teeth as well as intentions. "Can't say I'm surprised to see you, Char-o-lotte," he said, oozing out my name.

I raised an eyebrow, refusing to let this man intimidate me. He was the lowest form of trash. A man who preyed on those weaker. I knew it from firsthand experience. No matter what, I refused to react to his sleaze comments or innuendos. I'd faked my way through an on-screen kiss with a rather famous actor and his horrible halitosis, I could manage to sit with a handcuffed Boone without showing my disgust. "And why is that?"

"I imagine you're lonely with your man locked up," he said and laughed. "I'm willing to take Gett's sloppy seconds. Why don't you come give me a kiss?" He made kissing sounds, which grew louder and grosser when I failed to rise to the bait.

"Are you finished?" I asked after a full minute.

He shrugged. "I've got the time since I ain't getting out of here anytime soon."

"In that case, why don't you tell me what you were doing hanging around the Harker Motel on Saturday night?"

Eyes narrowing to mean slits, he growled, "You trying to pin something on me again?"

I frowned at the reminder of our last run-in a few months ago. Brodie and I had the unfortunate experience of visiting Boone at his home, if one could call it that rather than cesspool, during our attempt to save Jack from a murder charge. It was not a memory I wanted to revisit. "I'm merely asking a question," I said with a shrug.

"Well, I ain't gonna answer. Hear me?"

I ran my finger along the edge of the table, as if unconcerned. When in truth I regretted the action immediately. Who knew what sort of germs I'd just contracted. "Okay, if you say so."

"You should be talking to your own kin. Not me. I ain't killed nobody."

Acid burned in my stomach. "Are you referring to Evan? Did he say something to you about the murder?"

"I'm done answering your questions." He crossed his arms as well as one could with their hands cuffed to a table. "Unless you're willing to do a little something for me . . ." His eyes fell to my breast tucked away under my shirt. Bile rose quickly up my throat. Unable to help myself, I drew back. His laugh bounced around the small room. "That's what I thought. You have yourself a real nice day now, Char-o-lotte."

Chapter 33

Following my chat with Boone, I did what any woman forced to endure Boone's presence for longer than a minute would do, I ran home to shower. In very, very hot water. Once I dried off, I spent the next few hours straightening my room after the thief had wrecked it. This worked in two ways. Mindlessly cleaning helped me focus on the investigation so far, while it also allowed me to avoid talking to Jack about Evan's possible involvement in Marcus's murder.

After I dusted, vacuumed and polished every surface, only one option remained. I took a nap. I was being a coward, and I knew it. But having this sort of heart-to-heart with a man with a heart condition sounded about as fun as doing the little something Boone had requested.

When I could avoid it no longer, I started for the stairs, pausing at the top when Rue's voice reached me. She was sitting on the couch across from Jack's chair, a drink of Lucky in her hand. I smiled as she took a sip, giving an exaggerated grimace. "Next time, we're meeting at my house," she complained. "This Lucky tastes like lighter fluid."

Jack snorted. "Best-tasting lighter fluid in all of Florida, or so *Whisky Magazine* declared last year." He smiled, showing off white, albeit fake, teeth. "Or don't you remember?"

"You must've bribed the judges," she said in a loud voice. "That's the only explanation for it."

Jack set his own glass down. "Hush, woman. If Char catches us drinking off the small batch, she'll lock it up tight. That girl is a mean one."

Rue snorted, surprising me with the sound. "You are lucky she didn't take off with that Marcus Savage fellow. That's what you are."

"Don't I know it." I grinned at Jack's agreement. As I took the first step down the stairs, his next words stopped me. "I did what I had to do to keep Charlotte here. Given the same circumstances, I'd do it again without hesitation."

Bile rose up my stomach. What had Jack done? The bloodstained motel room swirled to mind. I came down the stairs, taking two at a time. Three steps from the bottom, my toe caught the edge of the step and I fell forward. My torso took the brunt of the impact, and I ended up sprawled on the ground at the bottom of the long flight of steps.

Jack peeked around his chair and shook his head. "I warned you about running down those steps like a loon."

I gave a gasped laugh. "Yes, you did. When I was ten."

"Point still stands," he said, deadpan.

I closed my eyes, trying to catch my breath. It bubbled somewhere between laughter and a groan. For the second time in a matter of hours, I'd taken a header down the steps. This time the fault was entirely mine. In a way, I was almost happy to have hit the ground, for the very idea of Jack killing Marcus had faded from my mind. While I didn't doubt he would kill for me, I couldn't see him, in his infirmed state, lifting the heavy lamp and crushing it against Marcus's skull. Furthermore, why would Marcus let Jack into his motel room at three in the morning? He wouldn't. Which meant Jack hadn't killed him.

Though it did leave me questioning just what Jack had actually done to keep me here. And more importantly, why were Rue and Jack acting as thick as thieves of late, older thieves who walked with canes, but thieves nonetheless.

Jack, if anything, was stubborn to the core. If he didn't want me to know something, then I'd never hear it from his lips. Which was the beauty of Gett in many ways. A secret was only secret for so long. My best bet was to ask Sweet Jayme to crack him. She merely had to look Jack in the eye with her nearly black gaze, and the truth would spill from his lips.

Especially after half a bottle of Lucky.

I grinned, happy to have a plan in mind that involved Jayme doing my dirty work. Jack could and would never stay mad at her. Sure, he'd lecture me for an hour, but never Jayme. Though, to be honest, she'd gotten me into way more trouble as a teen than I had her.

"Are you hurt, dear?" Rue asked after a few minutes of me still laying on the floor.

"No. Just thinking."

"That's nice," she replied.

I pulled myself up on my elbow. "Rue?"

"Yes?"

I swallowed. Giving an apology to a Gett rubbed against the grain. However, I owed her one, if not more. "I'm sorry I got you in trouble with your grandson."

She laughed. "I'm not the one in trouble, dear. Your sympathy belongs with Danny."

I tilted my head. "How so?"

"Marshall's making mushroom casserole for Sunday dinner."

Jack burst out laughing. I looked to him with question. "Everyone knows Danny's allergic to mushrooms."

I winced. Rue was one cold-blooded granny.

Rue laughed at my expression. "What Jack means to say is, he's mildly allergic. Gets a red, itchy rash. Nothing more. A fitting revenge for a man who raises his voice to the woman who practically raised him, don't you think?"

I did.

"And it's his own fault if he's too stubborn to admit to having an allergy. I don't force him to eat mushrooms."

I'd bet many a murderer had said as much. I didn't make him eat the poison . . .

I rose to my feet, brushing off my shorts. "I'm sorry just the same."

"I appreciate it, dear."

I licked my lips, unsure if I should ask her the question that had rattled around in my head since seeing the surveillance footage. "Do you know what Brodie was doing running around in Harker at three in the morning?"

She shook her head. "You should ask him."

I was afraid she'd say that. I turned to my grandfather, snatching the bottle of Lucky he had tucked into the side of the chair. "We need to have a talk about . . ." My eyes shifted to Rue, knowing she was listening to every word. "A few things." Top of the list was Evan. I also considered telling him about the bank's refusal to give us a loan too, but decided against it. There had to be a way to get enough cash to buy a new still.

The ring on my finger sparkled mockingly.

I gave it a hopeful tug, but it stayed firm.

My cell phone buzzed in my pocket. I pulled it free, checking the caller ID. "Brodie? Please tell me I'm not your one phone call."

He chuckled. "Not quite. But I do need a favor."

"Okay . . ." I agreed slowly.

"I need a ride back to Gett."

My eyes widened. "Danny let you go? Or is this more of a break-out-of-jail scenario?"

Another chuckle, this one more forced. "Somewhere between the two."

"I'll be there in thirty minutes."

"Thanks," he said. "As a thank-you, I'll buy you dinner."

My stomach growled in agreement. "See you in a few."

Chapter 34

After we hung up, I reheated Jack and Rue a salmon dish Sweet Jayme had kindly left for dinner. The fish smelled delicious, but was nothing in comparison to the whiskey and cinnamon sweet potato mash she'd made from scratch. A recipe handed down from her mother. I stopped myself from stealing more than a tablespoon of the warm, gooey goodness.

"Dinner's on the table," I told Jack as I gave my hair a fluff and reapplied a coating of lipstick. He slid Rue a knowing glance, which made me regret the action immediately.

"Give Brodie my love," Rue said with a laugh.

I stifled a sharp retort and left the house. Rue and Jack's laughter rang in my ears as I put the pickup into gear. The trip to the jail took me less than fifteen minutes. Brodie was waiting by the curb when I pulled up. He thanked me, jumping into the passenger seat. It groaned under his weight. "I'm starving," he said. "How does the Gett Diner sound?"

I nodded. While we would pass a bunch of better, healthier options on our way back to Gett, the diner felt like the safest option. We drove in silence. I spent the time gathering my courage enough to ask Brodie about the surveillance footage.

Before I broke the quiet with the question, he spoke. "I should've told you about my being in Harker around the time Savage was killed."

"Why didn't you?"

He hesitated for a moment, staring out the passenger window as the swampland flew by. "Because I knew how it would look. To you. To Danny. To everyone." He paused to blow out a breath. "I didn't kill him. I swear it."

"I know."

He turned his head my way. "You do?"

"I never thought you did."

His eyebrow rose.

"Fine," I said, turning my gaze back to the road. "I might've at first, but especially not now. Not after my chat with Boone."

"What?" he growled. "You talked to Boone without me? Do you have any idea how dangerous he is?"

"Not very with his hands cuffed to the table." I grinned at the memory. "But I'll admit, I'd have liked you there. He said some things . . ." I stopped. Boone wasn't what I wanted to talk about at this moment. And from the look on Brodie's face, neither did he. "Why did Danny let you go? When I talked with him, he was . . . less than convinced of your innocence."

He gave a laugh, but there was little humor in it. "Mindy Drift alibied me."

Something squeezed in my chest. A feeling I didn't like at all. Was I jealous? No, that couldn't be it. Brodie was free to sleep with whomever he liked. Heck, until a few days ago, I was engaged to another man. No way that I was jealous.

My face must've reflected my turbulent thoughts, for he said, "Get your mind out of the gutter, Charms. Mindy saw me running that morning, as she left from a . . . sleepover with someone, who is not me."

"Oh."

He shook his head, his cocky smile firmly in place. "Danny, who now has no suspects other than you, of course, was far more enthusiastic about my innocence."

"He can't still think I had something to do with the murder."

Brodie's shoulders lifted in a shrug.

My eyes drifted back to the road, and the fading light. The sky glowed orange, with hints of pink streaks. A pretty picture overall, but one that didn't fit with the topic at hand. "None of that explains why you were running around Harker at three in the morning."

For a long moment I didn't think he'd answer. This time the silence between us was fraught with meaning. I wanted to snatch back the question, to leave his secrets his own. Instead, I remained quiet, waiting. He released a harsh breath, his voice quiet. "Most nights I don't sleep. Haven't for almost a year." His hand went to his torso, where two bullets had destroyed his military career and nearly cost his life. "So I run."

I nodded, a lump forming in my throat. All the time he spent in the Gett Bar made a certain sort of sense now. With whiskey came sleep.

"Brodie, I—"

"Don't," he said quickly. "Please, don't."

I'd wanted to offer comforting, even encouraging words, but instead I said, "I was only going to ask if you wanted to shower off your jail stink before we had dinner."

A wide smile crossed his face. "Ms. Lucky, I'm shocked by your lewd suggestion."

I pressed my foot on the brake. "You know that I can leave you to walk back to Gett."

"That I do. That I do."

Chapter 35

An hour later, Brodie, his hair still wet from the shower, scooted across the blue vinyl of the booth. I did the same but on the opposite side. Cindy Mae, baby Cole caged in a Babyjörn attached to her, handed us a pair of sticky menus. The stickiness wasn't from the baby but rather a part of the diner's charm. Retro disgusting.

Thankfully the kitchen itself was spotless. Manny, the cook, wouldn't have it any other way. Which explained the scent of bleach wafting through the air under the mouthwatering aroma of French fries. "What'll you have?" Cindy Mae asked, uncharacteristically subdued.

My eyebrow arched. "Are you okay?"

With a sigh, she plopped down in the booth next to me. "My feet are killing me, and Cole's teething, so he's up all night. Colin's probably ready to leave us and I can't blame him." Tears leaked from her eyes.

Brodie shifted in his seat, as if uncomfortable with the topic. Odd since he had no problem discussing cold-blooded murder. I patted Cindy Mae's arm. "Colin loves you both. He's not going to leave you." I motioned to Brodie. "And if he does, Brodie would be happy to babysit all five kids while you're at work."

Brodie surprised me by nodding. "Not that Colin would dare leave your brood, but yes, I'd be happy to babysit."

"Oh, bless you," Cindy Mae said, already unstrapping Cole. She passed the baby to Brodie, who had little choice but to take the little bundle of joy in his arms. She quickly jumped from the booth, hurrying to the kitchen.

Brodie held Cole out, as if unsure what to do. "She didn't even take our order."

I laughed at his disgruntled tone. "I'm sure she'll be back soon. In the meantime, tell me all about your time in the slammer. Did you make any new friends?"

He snorted. "You're hilarious." Picking up his napkin, he wiped a spot of drool from the baby's mouth. "When I was teething, my mom would dab my guns with whiskey. The Lucky kind, of course. No use wasting good Gett."

"Explains a lot," I said, deadpan.

He pulled Cole to his chest, patting his back. I worried the kid would have bruises, but by the toothless laugh bubbling from Cole's lips he didn't mind the rough treatment. "Danny and Willow should have a few of these."

I choked on the water I'd just sipped. "Danny and Willow? I think you're jumping the gun a bit. Your brother doesn't give Willow the time of day."

"Us Getts, we're deliberate. Not slow." He grinned. "Danny will make his move, eventually."

"Like when Willow's in her seventies."

Brodie's eyebrow rose. "So you noticed how much time Jack and Rue have been spending together."

I shook my head, my stomach rebelling. "I do not want to talk about that."

A laugh burst from his lips, startling Cole, who let out a cry. Cindy Mae peeked her head out of the kitchen, and then slipped back behind the door. Brodie's laugh turned into a frown. "She's never coming back," he said, before adding, "If Jack and Rue's relationship isn't up for discussion, what do you care to discuss?"

"How about whether you think the paparazzo's attack is linked to Marcus's murder? Two men attacked at the same motel is too much of a coincidence to ignore, right?"

Brodie pulled Cole away, holding him eye to eye. "What's it about women and their desire to talk about murder on a date?"

"We. Are. Not. On. A. Date," I bit out.

"I'm buying you dinner, and I took a shower, even put on cologne." He sniffed his shirt. "Smells like a date." His nostrils flared and his eyes began to water, and Cole let out a baby giggle. "Never mind. The date smell is definitely gone."

I held my breath until the stench followed me across the table. "Want to bet Cindy Mae knew that was going to happen?"

"No bet." He rose from the booth, Cole still in his arms. With determined steps, he headed for the kitchen. A full minute later, Cindy Mae strolled out, minus her baby. Once again she sat down in the booth next to me, this time a wide smile on her face. "That man's too easy."

I laughed until tears came to my eyes. Cindy Mae joined in.

Once we sobered, she took my order, and then headed back to the kitchen. Brodie returned to the table a few minutes later, his hands suspiciously empty. "No tip for Cindy Mae," he said.

I couldn't help but laugh at his tone.

"Now where were we?" he asked once he sat. "Oh, right, we're about to have a pleasant meal while discussing the murder of your fiancé."

"Pleasant might not be the right word," I said as Cindy Mae came from the kitchen carrying two plates of the special—Chicken Fried Steak. She set them down in front of us, bowed mockingly, and left. I glanced at the gravy-soaked plate, said a silent prayer, and dug in. The first bite tasted like heaven. I took a second, and then a third, before speaking again. "Did you tell Danny about the intruder at my place?"

He shook his head. "Not yet. We weren't on the best terms when I left."

"Good."

His eyebrow rose.

"Not about the two of you, but about not telling him about the break-in."

"Why is that?"

I exhaled loudly. "Because I don't think the murder and the break-in are connected. Not anymore."

"Because of something Boone said? You're really going to believe that guy?"

I shook my head. "It's not about what he said, but about how well I know my cousin. More and more it feels like Evan knows more about the murder than he's told us." I filled him in on what Grace had said about the Honda and how the surveillance footage also caught a car leaving the motel parking lot around the time of the murder.

When I finished, he said, "Cheer up, Charms, it could be worse."

"How so?"

He finished his plate and pushed it away. "You could be Cindy Mae when she notices I used the last diaper in her diaper bag, and didn't tell her."

Chapter 36

Brodie paid the bill, leaving a large tip for Cindy Mae, I noticed. My eyebrow rose in question. "Just in case Colin really does leave. Don't sound so surprised," he barked when I snorted. "I occasionally do something nice."

"I'll believe it when I see it . . . for a second time."

"Come on," he said, motioning to the door. Before we reached it, it flew open, and in walked Mr. Burns and a woman who looked remarkably like him, I assumed to be his wife. "Oh," he said, blushing to the roots of his thin hair. "Hello, Ms. Lucky. Brodie."

"Good to see you, Wallace," Brodie said.

Wallace? Brodie was on a first-name basis with Mr. Burns? The very same banker who turned down my loan?

"Please give Rue our best and thank her for the lemon bars," Mrs. Burns said with a kind smile.

My gaze flew between Brodie and Mr. Burns, searching for the slightest sign of guilt at destroying our chance to buy a new still. When neither even flinched, I shook my head at my paranoia. And then Mr. Burns ruined it by saying, "Ms. Lucky, I'm glad I ran into you. I meant to offer my apologies for our conversation earlier."

My heart jumped. "Does that mean you can give us the loan?"

He was shaking his head before I finished my question. "I wish I could. But, frankly, with the incident . . . my hands are tied . . ."

Of course. Once the bank learned I was at risk to be arrested for murder, they pulled the plug on our loan. Rue and even Brodie had nothing to do with it. I blushed, my eyes lowering to the ground. "I understand." I slipped past the couple. "If you'll excuse me . . ."

Brodie came out a few seconds after me, his face flushed. "If there is anything I—"

I cut him off. "Act like you never overheard that conversation. Please?"

"Before I do, have you given any more thought to selling that ring?"

I ran my finger over the smooth surface of the largest diamond.

"Danny said he hasn't been able to track down any close relations for Savage." He picked up my hand, running his own thumb along the edge of the ring. "Why don't you let this ring do some good for you?"

I jerked my hand away. "I . . . Maybe you're right."

"I always am."

I rolled my eyes. "I think I'll drive up to Immokalee tomorrow, see if I can find a jeweler who wants to buy it." Not that Immokalee had a ton of options for fine jewelry. But it did have a few gold and jewelry pawn shops. The question was, would they have enough cash to buy an over-two-carat diamond once owned by a celebrity? If the jeweler didn't, maybe they knew someone who would.

His eye swept over my face. "I have something to get up there too. I might tag along."

I raised an eyebrow. "I don't need your protection, if that's what this is." Though, to be honest, I'd appreciate the company. I hated the drive across Gator Row. Not only was it more dangerous in the old pickup, but passing by the very place my parents perished so many years ago always sent a rush of wet, hot tears to my eyes. With Brodie riding shotgun, my mind would be on him, and his more annoying traits, than what could've been.

He scoffed. "You think I'm trying to protect you? A woman more than capable of taking care of herself?"

"Don't push it." I shook my head at his teasing grin. "I'll let you come, but only because the radio is broken, and I don't want to spend two hours listening to myself sing."

He laughed. "Having heard you sing I'd have to agree."

"You're not helping yourself."

"Forgive me." He bowed at the waist. "Now that that is settled, we should—"

The buzzing of my cell phone cut him off. Raising my hand in apology, I checked the caller ID. Unknown caller. "Hello?"

"Charlotte?"

I frowned, not recognizing the voice. "Yes?"

"Oh, good," the man said. "It's Pastor Matt."

"Yes, of course. Hello, Pastor." I paused. "What can I do for you?"

His voice, filled with warmth, was calming, like a promise that everything would be all right. Though I knew better than most how easy it was to fake that sort of reassurance. Actors did it all the time in commercials for life insurance. "Are you all right?"

"Yes, of course. Why?"

He hesitated. "This isn't my place, but such a great loss effects people in different ways. As you witnessed with Grace. I'm here if you need to talk."

"Thank you."

"There was another reason for my call. Have you thought more about if you want a service for Mr. Savage?"

I winced. I hadn't. Not one bit. Guilt burned in my stomach. If Marcus had no family, at least none Danny could find, wasn't it my duty to see to his memorial? Then again, one thing I'd learned about Marcus since his death was just how little I truly knew of him. Could I say for sure that he would want a small service in a town he visited for less than seventy-two hours before his death? "I don't think so," I said, "but I thank you for the offer."

"You are most welcome," he said. "Would you mind if I said a few words to the congregation about his loss on Sunday? Nothing too formal, just enough to provide closure for those who need it."

"That would be nice," I said, though I dreaded it. Having the town hate me for supposedly painting the water tower was one thing, but having them judge me for Marcus's murder would be more than I could take. Even more so since I was, in fact, innocent of both crimes.

"Good. Okay, then, it's settled." He hesitated again. "Have a good night."

"You too," I said, and then hung up. Brodie looked at me, his eyebrow raised in question. "Pastor Matt," I explained.

"I heard that part. What did the good man want?"

If I didn't know better, I'd think Brodie sounded jealous. "To ask about a memorial service for Marcus."

He ran his fingers along his cheek. "Not a bad idea."

"What? Why?"

"On those crime shows, the few you were in, didn't the murderer always attend the funeral?"

I shook my head. "Yes, on TV, they do. But this isn't fiction. It's real life. In case you've forgotten."

"Yeah, it must've slipped my mind," he said sarcastically. "In that case, let's go have a chat with Cousin Evan."

Chapter 37

As darkness claimed the sky, I drove along the rutted dirt road, careful to avoid any nocturnal wildlife. The Everglades had a split sort of personality. In the day, it buzzed with insect life, the snap of gator jaws, and the squawk of birds flying overhead. At night, under the cover of blackness, predators hunted, lying in wait for their next meal. As much as I hated the idea of being in the swamp during the day, being lost in it at night froze me in terror.

"Breathe," Brodie said from the seat next to me.

I inhaled and exhaled loudly before I realized I'd done it. "I'm fine. Just nervous about meeting with Evan."

"Really?" he asked as if he didn't buy it.

And I couldn't blame him. While I didn't necessarily want to accuse my cousin of murder, it didn't rattle me nearly as much as driving this close to the swamp at night. "Shut up," I snapped.

"Yes, ma'am."

We drove the rest of the way to Evan's trailer in silence, my hands red from gripping the steering wheel. As we pulled in next to Evan's trailer I noted the absence of his gold Honda. That and the fact the trailer was dark both told me he wasn't home. Whoever said this detective business was tough?

Brodie opened the passenger-side door, which groaned loudly. I winced at the grating sound in the stillness of the night. "He's not here," I whispered.

"I can see that," Brodie said. "I'm going to search his trailer."

"What?!" I shouted.

"Quiet," Brodie said. "I'll just be a minute."

I glanced to the darkness beyond the window and back to Brodie. Without a second thought, I leapt from the truck and followed Brodie toward the trailer. He stopped. "Where do you think you're going?"

I straightened. "With you."

"No."

"But—"

"Someone needs to look out in case Evan comes home."

The very idea of waiting outside, in the dark, with who knows what lurking nearby was enough to start my teeth chattering. I clamped down on them before Brodie heard the sound. "I don't like this," I said. "If Evan suspects someone broke in he's going to take off. And where would that leave us?"

"I doubt Evan would notice if his trash inside was disturbed." Brodie looked unconvinced. "How about this? If the door is unlocked, I'll slip in and take a quick look around."

"Okay," I agreed, following him to the door. "Try knocking first. Just in case he's inside, asleep."

He did as I suggested.

No answer.

As Brodie's fingers grasped the latch in the door, I held my breath. Please let it be locked, I thought. Luck was on my side, as the door stayed firmly closed. Brodie's face fell, and in that moment I understood him better than I had before. Brodie was bored. He missed the action of military life. He lacked purpose, a reason to wake up in the morning, or to get to sleep at night.

I squeezed his arm. "We can try again tomorrow. I'm sure Jack has a spare key to the trailer lying around somewhere."

His eyes narrowed with question.

"The trailer used to belong to my father. I spent my first few years of my life living inside."

"Oh," he said, his eyes filling with concern. "I didn't realize."

I hated the sympathy in them. It was the same look I saw in other people's gaze when they inevitably found out I was an orphan. "It's no big deal. I'll search for the key tomorrow, and we can check in to see if Evan is home after we get back from Immokalee."

"Sounds like a plan."

I blew out the breath I hadn't known I was holding. "Good. Now can we get back in the pickup before these mosquitoes eat me alive?" I swatted at an invisible pest to emphasize my point. Brodie saw right through me, if the smirk he shot me was any indication.

Chapter 38

I pulled up to Brodie's house around eight in the morning. Luckily his neighbor, Mrs. Branson, wasn't around. The less gossip about the two of us the better. Brodie came outside dressed in a gray T-shirt, worn nearly threadbare, and a pair of jeans. His dark hair was slicked back, wet from the shower. He took one look at the truck and said, "Why don't we take my Jeep?"

I tried not to take offense. Tried, but failed. "There is nothing wrong with my truck."

He grinned. "Other than the fact we probably won't make it fifty miles up the highway before it breaks down."

"Besides that," I groused.

"Come on, Charms." He motioned to the Jeep. "If you're nice, I'll share the basket of muffins I baked for us."

"When did you have time to bake muffins?" My eyes narrowed with suspicion. "I just decided to sell the ring last night."

"Fine. They're store-bought, but I did put them in the picnic basket all by myself."

I wasn't sure I believed him, but there wasn't any point in arguing. Or rather, it was too early to argue, especially since I hadn't finished a full pot of coffee just yet.

Once we settled on our mode of transportation, I leaned back in the soft fabric seat of the Jeep and closed my eyes. Before I knew it, I was fast asleep, the buzz of the Jeep's working radio droning in the background.

"Charms," Brodie said sometime later. "Hey, wake up. We're almost there."

I jerked awake with an admittedly unladylike snort.

He laughed. I threw him a disgruntled glare that he didn't even have the decency to notice. A few minutes later, we pulled into a blacktop parking lot with a sign that read *We Bye Gold & Jewelry*. The sign didn't instill confidence. "I know," he said with a grin. "We can always say bye-bye, if you don't get a fair price."

"You are hilarious."

With a chuckle he followed me into the shop. I stopped just inside the door, surprised by the neat and clean rows of pawned items. Plenty of gold and diamonds. So the sign outside wasn't completely off base. Musical instruments hung on the walls too. I smiled at a gleaming French horn, memories of the day Jack bought me a similar one filling me. I swear Jack had spent the next six months hiding in the distillery.

"I bet you two are looking for wedding rings." A man with tattooed arms and a heavy beard beamed at us. "I have just the set."

My face heated. "We're not . . . That's not why we're here."

His face clouded and then warmed with greed as his eyes fell on my finger. "That's quite a ring."

"Thanks," I said. "It's why we're here."

Brodie stepped forward, his hand on the small of my back. "We're interested in selling the ring, provided the price is right."

I sidestepped, glaring at Brodie. "Is it something you'd be interested in?"

The man motioned me forward as he reached for a jeweler's loupe. He pressed the magnifier to his eyes and took my hand in his, rolling it back and forth. The diamond sparkled like fire in the light. After a full minute, he released my hand and set down the loupe. He glared at Brodie before turning to me. "I'm sorry, miss, but I'm going to pass."

My heart sank. My desperation must've showed on my face, for Brodie stepped up to the counter, his muscles coiled tight. "Do you know anyone who can afford to buy it?"

The man's glower grew. "Oh, I can afford it."

"Then make an offer," Brodie snapped.

The man glanced to me, his voice low when he answered, "Fifty."

"Fifty grand isn't bad." Brodie nodded. "Charms? Do you want—"

"Fifty dollars. Not fifty grand," the man growled.

"What?" My mouth opened and then slammed shut. "Are you kidding me? This is a two-carat diamond."

Both Brodie and the man looked my way with equally sheepish expressions. "I am sorry, miss. But the diamond is a fake."

Chapter 39

"A good one," the man added with yet another angry look at Brodie.

"Stop glaring at me. I wasn't the one who gave it to her!" Brodie chewed on the edge of his lip. "Let me see it." Taking my hand in his, he twisted the band, and as he did so, the ring slid free.

I jerked back, surprised.

We looked at each other, and then to my finger, where the ring had rested for days. A greenish ring marred my skin, proving just how fake it had been.

"That son of a bitch," Brodie grumbled under his breath.

I shook my head. "Marcus couldn't have known."

Brodie nodded tightly. "If you say so."

"Do you know what this means?" I frowned at the ring. "We could be looking at his murder all wrong."

"Who knows when the ring was switched, if that's what happened."

"What do you mean?"

Before he could respond, his cell phone jangled to life. "It's Danny," he said as he answered. "Hey, brother, what's going on?"

I tapped my foot impatiently as they spoke.

"Wait, what?" Brodie frowned into the phone. "What cookies?" My stomach grumbled at the word, reminding me that Brodie hadn't made good on his muffin promise. "Don't touch them," he yelled, dragging me from my chocolate chip fantasy. "We'll be at your place in two hours. Don't move until we can talk."

He hung up, stuffing the phone and the fake ring in his pocket. He grabbed my arm and drug me from the pawn shop. "What's going on?" I asked, stumbling along behind him. "Brodie, please stop." He did, once we reached the side of his Jeep. He unlocked the door with his key fob and motioned me inside. "Brodie," I said again, and his eyes finally focused on me. "Tell me what's happening."

He licked his lips. "I'm really not sure. Danny called to tell me, and I quote, 'tell your girlfriend I can't be bribed with cookies, especially chocolate chip ones.'"

"What?"

He grinned without humor. "My response exactly. Apparently Danny found a plate of chocolate chip cookies on his porch when he came home this morning, with a note, from you."

"But I didn't . . ."

"I know," he said.

"Oh my God," I whispered.

Seconds later, we were speeding back to Gett, the only sound, tires eating up pavement.

Chapter 40

We arrived at Danny's cabin on the edge of the swamp exactly an hour and a half later. The cabin wasn't what I'd expected. The exterior was rustic but well-maintained, fitting the wildness of the landscape perfectly. Danny leaned against his wooden porch railing, one boot kicked over his other.

Brodie pulled to a stop, dirt kicking up under the Jeep.

"What's going on?" Danny asked when Brodie jumped from the driver's seat.

"You didn't touch those cookies?" he asked in lieu of answering his brother's question.

"When have you ever seen me eat chocolate chip cookies?" Danny shrugged. "You know me, I'm more of a snickerdoodle man."

From years of church picnics when Marshall would bake a special batch of snickerdoodles for Danny, I knew that too. Brodie didn't smile at his brother's statement.

"I'm thinking those cookies might be bad for my health to boot," he drawled, gesturing to the plate, and the dead ants scattered around it.

Brodie bobbed his head, eyes burning. "Looks that way. Did you call it in?"

"Yeah," Danny said. "The crime techs will be here shortly."

I glanced between the brothers, noting their similarly cold eyes. And yet, to the outside observer, by the tone of their voices, nothing appeared out of the ordinary. Like someone tried to poison Danny every day, which now that I thought about it, wasn't that much of a stretch. "I can't believe someone is trying to frame me by killing your brother," I said, my arms on my hips, "and you two are standing around chatting as if we're talking about the weather."

"Just how do you want—" Danny began.

Brodie cut him off with a look. "I want to see the note."

With a glare at me, he reached into his pocket, pulling out an evidence baggy with a piece of paper inside. The plastic gleamed in the sunlight. "It's on Lucky Whiskey stationery."

"I didn't . . . you can't think that I wrote it."

One of his dark eyebrows arched.

"Of course he doesn't think that," Brodie said.

Danny tried and failed to stifle his grin. "At least not completely."

Brodie scowled at his brother. "This is no time for jokes. Someone wants you dead, and wants Charms in trouble for it. The question is, who?"

"I'd also like to know why. At least to the murdering me part."

Brodie stared at the note through the glare of the plastic bag. After a full minute, he spoke. "That's not Charms's handwriting. The letters are too ridged, hers are much loopier."

"We already established the fact it wasn't me," I said with annoyance.

"What I meant was, whoever wrote the note wasn't interested in copying your handwriting." He tapped the plastic bag, his eyes on his brother. "Have you annoyed anyone enough to want you dead lately? Other than Charms, that is. Have you made a questionable arrest? Pissed off a lover?"

Danny snorted. "Leave my love life out of this. While I arrest people all the time, I can't think of any who had access to Lucky stationery too, except for Evan Lucky."

Brodie's head shot up. "What?"

"I just sent a couple deputies to his trailer with an arrest warrant." Danny's lips thinned. "I shouldn't tell you this, but financial records came back on Savage's credit cards. There is a charge for a known bookie on it. A charge made after Savage's murder that was traced back to Evan. The judge signed off on a warrant last night." He paused. "And this morning, a plate of poisoned cookies arrives on my doorstep with that note."

"Couldn't that be a coincidence? Maybe this has nothing to do with Marcus. Your brother is quite unpleasant. He probably has hundreds of enemies."

"I wouldn't say hundreds," Danny said with a scowl that highlighted my point.

Brodie hid a smile. "True. But you don't honestly believe this is a coincidence, do you?"

I let out a harsh sigh. "No. Things like that only happen in the movies."

"Exactly." Brodie turned to his brother. "I'm guessing Evan wasn't home when the deputies went to arrest him."

"Nope, he surely wasn't." Danny hesitated. "We're trying to track down his whereabouts, but so far, no luck. But I *will* find him, and when I do—"

I cut him off. "You'll let Brodie and I talk to him."

"Are you kidding me?" Danny growled, tugging at the whiskers on his chin. "I would rather—"

"Just agree to what she wants. I'm finding things are easier that way," Brodie said with a long-suffering sigh. A sigh I didn't buy for a second. He wanted Danny to agree, wanted it so much his body almost vibrated with the desire. "Unless you want Charms running around town, sticking her nose in your investigation . . ."

Danny snorted, in what sounded an awful lot like appreciation. "Resorting to blackmailing your own brother. Is that how it is?"

"I learned from the best."

"Rue," the brothers said at the same time.

"Fine," Danny said. "When we have Evan in custody, I'll let you talk to him."

"Then we will leave you to your hunt." Brodie motioned me to the Jeep. I reluctantly followed, wondering if Danny hadn't planned this all along to keep us out of his hair.

Chapter 41

"Hey, Char-girl," Jack said as I walked through the door to the Lucky house. Brodie followed behind. Once he cleared the doorway, I flipped the dead bolt on the door. "You have to keep the doors locked," I reminded Jack, for what felt like the twentieth time.

He snorted. "As long as I've lived in this house, ain't nobody come inside without my permission."

I wanted to argue. I really did. But the truth would only upset him, and I didn't want to do that. Not yet. Learning the truth about Evan would be hard enough. Brodie and I shared a glance, his gaze imploring me to speak up, to tell Jack what we knew. I ignored him.

Thankfully he didn't take it upon himself to mention Evan's crime spree, for which I was extremely grateful. "What brings you by, boy?" Jack asked him. "Sick of that Gett swill? Ready to try the good stuff?"

Brodie grinned. "Rue would disown me for telling such a lie."

Jack laughed, swatting his knee, until his eyes watered. "Come, have a seat and tell me what you and my granddaughter have been up to. I bet it ain't no good."

"Can't right now," Brodie said. "Charms asked me to fix something in her bedroom."

My granddad's eyebrow rose. "Is that so?"

"Um, sure." A blush heated my face.

Brodie smirked. "I'm real handy."

"Shut up," I whispered, eyeing Jack. Thankfully his hearing wasn't what it used to be.

"That's no way to talk to a guest," Jack admonished. Brodie burst out laughing, and Jack joined him. Once they sobered, I led Brodie up the stairs to my bedroom. Thankfully I'd straightened the worst of the mess yesterday. Brodie stood at the threshold, a smile on his face.

"What?"

His grin widened. "Do you know how many times I dreamed of being right here, in Lucky Charms bedroom, when we were in high school. And now, it's a fantasy . . . turned nightmare." He ran his finger down the neon pink painted wall. "Is that a poster of Robert Pattinson?"

My cheeks grew hotter. "He's a talented actor."

"Uh-huh." He stepped further into the room, and in that moment, I saw it through his eyes. The room, much like the rest of the house, was stuck in the past. This room was trapped around 2009 or 2010, when I left for college. Jack hadn't changed a thing, and neither had I since returning home nine months ago. Maybe it was easier to live in the past, a place where I was safe from having to make the big decisions. "Nice dust ruffle." He pointed to the bed.

"Are you done?"

"Not quite."

I crossed my arms, glaring until his face lost any semblance of humor.

"Fine," he said with a sigh. "Let's get on with it. Tell me how the room looked when you first walked in."

I reached in my pocket for my phone. "I can do better than that." Flipping through photo after photo backed up to the cloud, I handed Brodie the phone when the first image of the destruction came into view. He held up the phone, as if memorizing the differences. I stayed quiet while he worked it out in his mind. He swiped across the screen to view each picture in super slow motion. With each passing minute, my anxiety grew. I paced in front of him, back and forth.

His finger swiped the opposite way, and he frowned.

"What?" I asked as his face looked grim.

"Nothing. Forget it." He handed me back my phone, and I glanced down at the picture he'd just viewed. It was one of the last ones Marcus and I had taken together, a shot of the two of us at Jack's party, Marcus wearing a smile that filled his face. Minutes later, I'd find his fake engagement ring on my finger. My thumb caressed the greenish skin on the space where the ring had circled my finger.

"From the photos, it doesn't look like anything was seriously damaged, except for your iPad." Brodie ran his hand along his jaw as he sat on the twin bed. It groaned under his weight. "What do you make of that?"

I glanced to the place on the floor where I first saw my broken iPad. "I didn't think anything of it, until you mentioned it. But you're right. Things were tossed around, as if searched, but nothing was broken other than the iPad." I tilted my head. "Do you think that really means something?"

He shrugged. "I have no clue. But it's a place to start. Do you still have it?"

I nodded, moving to the nightstand next to him. My breath caught in my throat as his presence threatened to overwhelm me. His physical strength felt too intimate in my childhood room. I inhaled sharply, then released the breath. He looked up at me with a question. I shook my head. I pulled the iPad free from the nightstand, handing it to him. The screen was cracked in the center, as if stabbed with some object in a fit of rage.

He held it out, turning it over. "Does it boot up?"

I shook my head.

"Anything important on it? Something Evan would want to destroy?"

I thought of Jack's will, which Jack and I had updated when I came home months ago. Jack had wanted to keep the distillery in Lucky hands after his death. Though I hadn't wanted to discuss the possibility of his leaving this earth, I'd done what he'd asked. "Maybe." I explained to Brodie about the will. "But Evan had to know that destroying my iPad wouldn't make the will disappear. Everything nowadays is backed up to the cloud."

"Good point," he said, once again turning it over. "So why else would he have trashed it?"

I sat on the bed next to him, staring at the cracked screen until my eyes glazed over. Not a single reason popped into my head. It made no sense. Unless he'd done it for no reason, but rather for the sheer pleasure. Evan hated me. Would it be that much of a stretch for him to enjoy wrecking my iPad?

"Charlotte," Sweet Jayme called from the steps below. I jumped away from Brodie, as if we'd been engaged in something more illicit than contemplation.

"Yeah?" I yelled back, my face feeling like it was on fire. He laughed, which didn't help. I shoved at his shoulder.

"Would you and Brodie like some lunch? I'm making plant-based burgers."

Jack's groan echoed all the way upstairs. Brodie's own joined his. I shot him a glare. "They taste better than the real thing."

He snorted.

"Yes, Jayme, we'd love too." I smiled sweetly at him while I yelled down to the kitchen.

"When this is over, Charms, I'm going to make you pay for that."

Chapter 42

Brodie sat in the kitchen, his eyes shooting daggers at me as the room filled up with the scent of plant-based protein in a frying pan. Sweet Jayme tried her best to stifle her laugh. "It's not that bad, Brodie Gett," she admonished. "Jack has come to even enjoy them."

"Everyone loves the taste of hockey pucks," Jack said with a wink.

"Don't encourage him," I said to my grandfather. "There is nothing wrong with replacing red meat with a healthier alternative."

Brodie's eyebrow inched up. "I'll remember that next time you order a hamburger with a side of fries at the Gett Diner."

I cleared my throat, changing the subject. "Jack, have you heard from Evan today?"

"No, why do you ask?"

"Evan . . . he . . ." The words died on my lips.

Brodie came to my rescue, though he looked far from happy about it. "I loaned him an adze, and I need it back before Rue finds out. We went to his trailer but he wasn't home."

Jack's weathered face wrinkled more. "We have plenty of our own coopering tools here. Why would Evan borrow one from you?"

"Not sure. But I really do need it back. It's been in our family since the early 1900s."

I stared at Brodie, shocked at how easily he could lie.

"When I talked to Evan yesterday he didn't say nothing about any tool." Jack shrugged. "But he was in a rush."

"Is that so?" Brodie tilted his head. "Any idea why?"

Jack took a sip from the glass of water on the table in front of him, grimacing slightly. For a man who once drank Lucky with every meal, being reduced to water consumption had to hurt. And he made it known to everyone around. I smiled at his displeasure. "Not a clue, but he sure was angry at you, Char-girl."

"Me?" I held my hand in front of me, like I was shocked by the news. When, in fact, his trashing my bedroom and trying to frame me for killing Danny was more than my first hint at Evan's anger.

"Did he say why?" Jack licked his lips while avoiding my eyes. A bad feeling ran up my spine. "Jack?"

"All right. All right. Don't get all huffy." He tossed the napkin he'd been holding to the table. "Evan came over to ask for money. I told him no, like you said."

"Jack . . ." I didn't quite believe him. "How much did you give him?"

He sighed. "A few hundred. Wasn't much, but it was all I had. He wasn't happy with it. When he left, he said to tell you . . . well, let's just say a gentleman doesn't speak that way."

Brodie laughed. "You sound just like Rue . . ." As he said it, his face paled. "Was she here when Evan was here?"

I knew just how he felt. The idea of Jack being alone, or even almost alone, with Evan made my heart thunder. Who knew what Evan was truly capable of at this point?

Jack's cheeks reddened. "What business is that of yours, boy? Your grandmother can do or see whoever she wants, whenever she wants."

Brodie had the grace to flush.

I came to his rescue as he'd done for me earlier. "Brodie isn't concerned with why Rue was here. He just wants to find Evan. Very badly."

Brodie nodded. "Jack, if you know anything about where he might be . . ."

"You didn't loan him an adze, did you?" Jack said quietly. "What's going on, Char?"

I glanced to Brodie, my eye imploring him to get up and leave so I could talk to Jack alone. He started to stand when Sweet Jayme's words stopped him. "Charlotte, do you know what's in this bottle? There's no label on it, and I've never seen it before." She hesitated. "It looks sort of like nutmeg, but doesn't smell right."

Brodie leapt from his chair, knocking it into the wall. I too jumped up, running to the cupboard where Sweet Jayme stood, a glass spice bottle in her hand. Brodie reached her first. Wrapping his hand in the bottom of his T-shirt, he snatched the bottle away from her. I took her hands in mine and led her to the sink to wash.

"What's wrong?" she whispered.

I glanced back at Jack, who sat in his chair, concern filling his face. I gave him a measured smile, which I then turned on Sweet Jayme. "Smile," I told her, motioning to Jack. She did as I asked. "I want you to wash your hands really good, and then take Jack into the living room. I'll be out in a minute to explain." Right after I called Danny. Hopefully his crime scene technicians already had an idea of what was in the cookies, and whether or not we needed to be worried about exposure. I dialed Danny's cell number while Brodie carefully placed the bottle in a plastic bag. He then washed his hands for a full minute.

After I hung up with Danny, who was already on his way here along with two deputies and an ambulance, I grabbed a bottle of Lucky from the cupboard, poured two healthy fingers of amber goodness into a matching pair of Scooby-Doo plastic cups from my childhood. The labels had long ago faded, leaving the vaguest outline of Shaggy and Scooby. I passed Brodie one, and drained the other.

He took a tentative drink, gave an exaggerated grimace, and set the cup down. "I guess we now know why Evan really broke in."

I nodded slowly, letting the warmth of the whiskey replace the coldness seeping into my bones. Had Jayme not found the bottle when she did, who knows what might've happened. "We have to find him."

"Give Danny a chance. If Evan is still hanging around Gett, which I doubt, Danny will find him."

I didn't share his confidence in his sibling, but I decided to drop the subject, for now. It wasn't like I had a better idea of where to find Evan anyway.

Sirens screamed on the road leading to my driveway. And a few minutes later, the Lucky living room exploded with cops, medics, and guys in crime scene jackets. Jack sat quietly in his chair, his eyes burning into my back. So far I'd avoided telling him the truth about Evan, but that didn't seem possible anymore. Much too soon, I'd have to sit my grandfather down and explain how the boy he'd known for the last twenty-two years wasn't the man he believed him to be.

And instead was a psychopath bent on murder.

143

Chapter 43

Hours later, in the dark of night, Danny and his deputies finally pulled away, the spice bottle cataloged and collected. Jack had a million questions, none of which I wanted to answer. Not yet at least. Once Danny caught Evan, and I had a chance to question him, then I might have the answers to satisfy the question of why.

Until then Brodie would be crashing on our couch. His stipulation, not mine. I reluctantly agreed, and he headed off to his place to pack a bag. Jack and I watched him drive off. "That Gett boy is one of the good ones, girl."

"What's your point?" I knew Brodie was a good guy. He'd been nothing but helpful since I all but accused him of murder.

Jack shrugged. "He'd be good to have around. On a regular basis."

"What?" Was this Jack's way of playing matchmaker? I didn't like that one bit. Whatever was or wasn't between Brodie and me was no one's business but ours. Not that there was such a thing as *our* business. That would imply we were more than . . . whatever it was we were.

"Something to think about," he said, turning to go back into the house, his cane tapping the ground in a rat-a-tat pattern. The sound continued long after Jack had shut the door behind him. "Shit," I cursed. The sound wasn't coming from Jack's cane, but from inside the distillery. The still again. If I didn't fix it in time the heat would build and build.

I ran toward the pulsing sound, praying I'd be able to shut it down before it blew, ruining our latest batch and maybe taking out one of the other stills. Flinging open the door to the still room, a blast of heat caught me full in the face, sending my hair curling under the humidity. Steam swirled around the room, making it hard to see more than a foot in front of me. Feeling my way along the outside wall, I located the master switch and flipped it off. The busted pipe hissed as the pressure faded.

I stepped inside the room to assess the damage, waving a hand in front of my face to dispel the worst of the steam. I froze when a voice reached me through the haze.

"Hello, Charlotte. I've been waiting for you."

"Evan?" Fear turned my voice harsh. I squinted until he came into view. What I saw then switched plain old fear to outright terror. In his left hand, he held a revolver, hung low at his side. I supposed I should be thankful it wasn't pointed directly at me but I wasn't. Not one bit. "What are you doing?"

He glanced down to the weapon, and then up at me, face grim. "I saw all the cops outside. Did you send them after me too?"

"Send them after you? Are you joking?"

"Why did you have to turn Marcus down?" he asked rather than answer.

My forehead wrinkled. What did my breaking off the engagement have to do with anything? "Evan, please, listen to me. For Jack's sake, stop this craziness. Give up before you or . . ." I glanced down to the gun. "Someone else gets hurt."

"It's not fair." He frowned, waving the gun in front of him. "I was here for Jack after you left for LA. I was the one who listened to his stories about his perfect Char-girl. And what did I get for spending time with him?"

Considering how many checks Jack had written him for gambling debts and other bills, I'd say he'd gotten plenty. His sense of entitlement made me reckless. "How about the love of a man who overlooks your spoiled-rotten personality traits."

"How dare you." The gun inched higher, and higher. Was this it? Was this how it ended for me? Unlucky enough to be killed by a Lucky? And here I thought Brodie Gett would be the death of me.

Before I could formulate a plan to escape, the busted pipe exploded with mist once more, filling the small room with steam. A blur of black whizzed through the door. Evan yelped, and a gunshot pierced the air. "Charms! Run!" Brodie screamed.

A second gunshot followed.

I debated doing what Brodie ordered, but it was as if my legs were frozen in place in the mist. I couldn't move. Couldn't even scream as I watched Brodie fight for both of our lives. He pulled back his fist, but not quickly enough. Evan pulled the trigger.

Chapter 44

"Next time I tell you to run, you better listen," Brodie said fifteen minutes later. He held a freezer-burned steak to the welt under his eye, while pinning me with a dark stare.

"If it will make you feel any better, the next time someone holds me at gunpoint, I will do exactly as you order." I hesitated. "Unless you're the one with the gun. Then I'm going to do the opposite of whatever you request."

"I'll remember that." He winced, shifting his weight on my kitchen chair. The medics had used the kitchen as a triage center, tending to Brodie's cuts and bruises, along with a broken rib, as well as Evan's more serious wounds. Brodie had dislocated my cousin's shoulder while adding in a concussion for good measure. All of which he'd deserved and more.

If it hadn't been for Brodie . . . I shuddered to think of what might have happened.

"You really should get that rib checked out," I said.

"Not going to happen. I can't trust you alone. Look what happened when I left for ten minutes. You almost got yourself killed."

My face heated. "How was I to know that Evan was hiding in the distillery? Wasn't it your brother's job to check to make sure he wasn't here?"

"Damn right it was." He frowned. "Danny and I will be talking that over, in six to eight weeks."

My forehead wrinkled. "Why wait so long?"

"That's how long it will take for my rib to heal."

"I don't under . . . Don't you dare!" I said. "I was kidding. Danny isn't at fault. Evan knows the distillery better than Jack does. He could've stayed hidden for weeks without anyone the wiser."

Brodie pulled the steak from his eye. "Then why didn't he?"

"What?"

"Why did he come after you?"

I shrugged. "I guess we'll find out when I talk to him."

"We."

"What?"

146

"When *we* talk to him."

I wanted to argue, but seeing the glazed look of pain in Brodie's eyes had me reevaluating. I blew out a long breath. "Fine. When *we* talk to him."

"Thanks."

I passed him a glass half full of Lucky's small batch. Guaranteed to fix whatever ailed you. Or at least make you forget about them for the moment. "I am the one who should be thanking you. How did you know Evan was inside the distillery?"

"I didn't. Not really."

"Then . . ."

He took a long swallow of the whiskey, not even bothering to give his typical affected grimace. "On my way to my place, I spotted Evan's Honda hiding in the swamp. I turned around, heading for the distillery." He frowned. "Of course, I didn't expect to see you inside, with a gun at your head."

"Torso."

"Excuse me?"

I sighed, wishing I'd never said it. Brodie's jaw was already clinched tight. Any more and he would need dental work. "The gun was pointed about here." I motioned to my midsection. "But that's not really my point. I owe you my life."

His face grew red, which made me laugh. "Keep it up."

"I'm glad about one thing." I took a drink of my own glass of Lucky. The warmth spread through me like a hug.

He tilted his head, the welt under his eye blackening rapidly. "What's that?"

"No one will be trying to kill us or frame me for murder any longer."

His eyebrow rose. "I wouldn't be so sure, Charms. Not with your luck."

Chapter 45

The next morning, I met Brodie at the Gett Diner before we drove to the sheriff's station to talk to Evan. Cindy Mae, her arms heavy with a tray of food, smiled as I walked in. Several of the other diners also glanced my way, with their usual accusatory stare.

Except for one friendly face.

I gave Pastor Matt, who was sitting with a group of church ladies, a wave, and headed toward the table in the back where Brodie sat, a cup of steaming coffee in front of him.

He looked up as I approached. My stomach dropped. His eye had swollen shut in the course of the night, which emphasized the blackness circling it. "You should be at home, resting," I said. "Does it hurt?"

He chuckled. "Only when I look at something. Stop staring at me like that."

"Like what?"

"Like it's all your fault. It isn't. Just like the last time."

Last time? The vaguest of memories flickered through my mind. We were in high school, the Monday after the homecoming dance. A dance I would never remember after my date failed to show up, leaving me sitting home alone. A purple and black bruise had circled Brodie's eye then too. I'd assumed the injury was from the game. I started to ask him what he meant, but Pastor Matt interrupted. "I'm so glad you're all right." He looked to Brodie and back at me. "Both of you."

"That makes three of us." I smiled at him, noting the lines around his eyes. Tending to one's flock, especially in a place like Gett, had to take a toll. While most folks went to church on Sundays, the rest of the week they were hardly the most pious. Myself included.

In fact, lately I'd had numerous impure thoughts. Too many about the man sitting across from me. And only half of those involved holding a pillow over his face.

"Do you mind if I sit for a moment?" Pastor Matt asked. "If I have to discuss the church's bake sale for one more minute, I will scream."

"Please do," I said.

Brodie's uninjured eyebrow rose, and I realized how that sounded. "I meant, please have a seat. Not to scream."

The pastor sat with a grateful smile. "Thank you. While I appreciate the ladies' hard work, deciding who makes the best chocolate chip cookie is hardly in my wheelhouse." He let out a small laugh. "I know. I know. It's a tough job, but someone has to do it. Thankfully that matter has now been put to rest. But enough about my trivial complaints. How are you holding up?" He patted my arm with concern.

"I'd be better if I had some answers about Marcus's murder," I said quickly.

"I do hope you find the answers you seek."

"Thank you."

We chatted for a few more minutes, and then he left. Brodie stared at his departing back. Cindy Mae came and took our order, and a few minutes later loaded plates arrived at the table. We dug in, enjoying the meal and quiet, as if each of us longed to avoid any more talk of murder.

When we finished, Brodie broke the peace. "I wonder if Danny searched Evan's trailer yet?"

"Probably. Why?" I glanced up from the steaming cup of coffee in my hand.

"Not sure." He shook his head. "Are you ready to go?"

I nodded, waiting as he placed two twenties on the table to cover our breakfast and coffee, plus a nice tip. I wanted to offer to pay, but then remembered my empty wallet. My expression must've belied my thoughts, for he reached for my arm. "Hey, Charms," he said, voice low.

I didn't want his sympathy, not again.

Waving to his swollen eye, he said, "Maybe you should drive."

Chapter 46

The pickup rattled as I stepped on the brake, but eventually stopped with a foot to spare before we ran into the yellow-painted cement barricade on the ground. Brodie's face regained some of its color as he stepped onto the blacktop of the sheriff's office parking lot. The ride over had been a bumpy one. Every time we hit a pothole or rut in the road, he'd grabbed his ribs and sucked in a breath.

After my fifth apology he'd vowed to jump the next time I showed a bit of sympathy. For the rest of the trip, I stayed quiet, only internally wincing along with him.

"What are you doing here?" Danny said as we walked into the sheriff's office.

Brodie's eyebrow hitched. "Why wouldn't we be here? You did say we could talk to Evan."

"That was before . . ." He waved toward Brodie's face. "The DA would kill me if I put you in a room with him."

A flush rose on Brodie's skin. I stepped between the brothers before an argument ensued. "But I can still talk to him, right? I mean, I am his only living relative besides Jack." When he started to deny my request, I added, "Surely no one could have a problem with that."

"This way," he said, motioning down the corridor. I glanced at Brodie to gauge his reaction, but nothing showed on his face. I followed Danny along the gray-walled hallway, pausing outside the interrogation room where I'd chatted with Boone a few days ago.

"Don't ask him anything about last night in case we have to call you as a witness." His voice lowered, "And, for the love of God, don't tell him anything about our case against him." He ushered me inside. Evan sat in the hard plastic chair. Unlike Boone his hands were not cuffed to the table. Instead one hand was cuffed to the chair and his other was resting in a sling. His eyes were red from crying, and his face looked pale and scared. Not what I expected from a cold-blooded killer.

He glanced up when I entered, more tears spilling down his cheeks. "Thank God you're here, Charlotte." He bawled. "You have to tell them that I'm no killer. Please. Help me."

Danny let out a dark chuckle. "Have fun," he said as he shut the door behind me. I sat on the chair opposite Evan, studying him. Did he actually think I'd help him after he nearly killed me last night? I asked as much, my voice filled with bitterness at the memory of the moments when I thought Brodie would die at his hand.

Rue would surely never have forgiven me for Brodie's death.

"That wasn't my fault," he whined. "Gett jumped me for no reason. I didn't even know it was him. Not at first. I thought it was . . . someone else."

"Who?"

He shook his head. "It doesn't matter. But you have to know that I would never hurt anyone, especially you. You're my blood."

I didn't buy it. Not one bit. "Tell me about Marcus. Why did you do it?"

His gaze lowered to the tabletop, where he traced a finger along it. "I didn't want to but he insisted. I'm real sorry, Charlotte."

Again with the mysterious person. "Who is *he*, Evan?"

His eyes widened. "Marcus, of course. It was all his idea."

I drew back, my head swimming. "What? You want me to believe that Marcus had some sort of death wish?"

"What?" He frowned. "I wasn't confessing to the *murder*! Are you listening to me at all?" he barked. "I already told you, I didn't kill or attempt to kill anyone."

"Except you did. Last night." I ran my hands over my arms as a chill slipped over my body. "But let's say I believe you, why would you hide in the distillery if you're innocent?"

He tried to wipe a tear from his face but the handcuffs prevented it. "I wasn't hiding from the cops, but from . . . Oh, the hell with it. I was trying to avoid running into Boone."

"Did he kill Marcus?"

"What?" He shook his head. "Why would Boone kill Marcus?"

"You just said . . . Never mind. Why were you avoiding Boone?" A headache pounded at my temples. I rubbed them for a moment, before looking back up at my cousin.

"Because of you," he yelled, his face growing red. "Whatever you said to him made him mad. At me. When he got out of jail, he called and threatened me. I did the only thing I could think of. I packed a bag and bunked down in the rackhouse. I would've stayed inside, but I heard the still blow, and went to fix it. That's when you came in."

"But you had a gun!"

"For my own protection," he snapped.

I opted not to argue the point. "You said Marcus insisted you do something. What was it?"

"Promise you'll try and get me out of here?"

I nodded, though I had zero intention of helping him escape justice.

"Marcus promised to cut me in on a deal he had going. If I'd do something for him." He hesitated. "At first I told him no. You have to believe me."

I didn't. Not one bit.

"Eventually, though, he talked me into it."

"Into what?"

"Keeping Brodie Gett far away from you. Not that I could, even if Marcus hadn't promised me a ton of money. I did everything I could think of to keep Gett away. Had Mindy flirt with him at Jack's party. Nothing. I even stabbed the tires on his Jeep. But it didn't slow him down."

My eyes narrowed, pinning Evan in place. "But why? Why did he want to keep Brodie from me?"

"So Marcus could gain control of Lucky."

I snorted. "Over my dead body."

"Not dead." His eyes darkened. "But married. Marcus figured Brodie was the only obstacle in his way."

Chapter 47

I stood in the hallway outside the interrogation room, taking slow, calming breaths. In truth, I wanted to run back into the room and attempt my very own murder. Cousinicide sounded pretty good about now. Blood to Evan hadn't been nearly as thick as the whiskey business or the promise of cash. I wasn't so much surprised by his lack of loyalty as I was about Marcus's plan. For one thing, Marcus was fairly well-off, at least by Gett standards. It wasn't like Lucky Whiskey was worth a bunch of money. And certainly not enough to marry me. So why the ruse? What could Marcus have hoped to gain?

"All finished?" Brodie asked as he came up behind me.

I visibly jumped, and then blushed. "Stop sneaking up on me."

Grinning, he motioned to his thick-soled boots. "A deaf elephant could hear me in these things."

"Did you just imply that I am fat?"

"What? No. What?" He squirmed, which more than made up for his having snuck up on me in the first place. I decided to let him off the hook. "I'm kidding."

"You are a cruel one, Charms. I'd do well to remember that."

"Not enough to keep gold diggers at bay."

He tilted his head. "How's that?"

"I'll explain later. But first, I need to talk to your brother." Brodie followed me down the corridor to the open-air offices of the bullpen. Danny sat inside the only office with walls, albeit glass ones. I motioned for him. He ignored me, turning in his chair to give us his back.

Rather than play his childish game, I yanked open his door and stepped inside before he could protest. "I need to talk to you."

"I'm busy. Though Luckys account for a large percentage of transgressions in these parts, I do have other crimes to solve."

"You're hilarious."

"Give Charms a minute of your precious time. You owe *me* that much," Brodie said, lifting his hand to his blackened eye. Danny's face changed, going from thin-lipped annoyance to genuine regret. I hated for Brodie to use his injury to gain Danny's cooperation. But seeing as it worked so well, I was happy to rub it in a bit more.

"Your brother could've died . . ." When Danny glared at me, I shrugged. "Too much, huh?"

"A little," Brodie said with a grin.

"You have fifty seconds left," Danny growled. "So talk fast."

I rolled my eyes, but did as he asked. "You pulled credit reports on Marcus, right?"

"What of it?"

"Did they . . . was he . . ."

"Thirty-eight seconds," Danny said.

Brodie shook his head. "Sorry my brother's such an ass. It's not genetic."

I cleared my throat to stop any further sibling snipping. "How in debt was Marcus?"

Danny opened a file drawer, pulling out a thick manila folder. A stack of papers sat inside, along with some gruesome crime scene photos. I looked away as my stomach rolled. He finally let out a grunt, indicating he'd found what he was searching for. I glanced back, happy to see the photos had vanished.

"Here it is," he said. "Damn."

"That bad, huh?" Brodie said in a suspiciously cheerful tone. I shot him a glare, then returned my attention to Danny, who was reading the report. When he finished, he looked up.

"He owed over a million dollars to various credit cards, as well as a few unsecured loans. Are all Hollywood people so reckless with their money?"

My face heated. Lucky Whiskey, no matter how you looked at it, was in deep financial straits, and it was my fault. Was I too reckless? Or was I not aggressive enough? Maybe I needed to chat with Mr. Burns again, lay out my case, and insist we get a loan, no matter at what percentage rate. Even as the thought crossed my mind, I shook it off. While it wouldn't hurt to approach Mr. Burns again, I wouldn't indebt Lucky for life. There had to be another way.

Evan's words about Marcus wanting Lucky flickered through my head again. Why would a man, already in debt up to his chiseled chin, want the added burden of a nearly bankrupt distillery in a backwater town?

Maybe it wasn't him who had wanted it.

Maybe, just maybe, someone else wanted it enough to buy it from Marcus, regardless of the price. And when I refused to marry Marcus, it all but signed his death warrant.

But who would want Lucky so badly?

Only one person came to mind.

Chapter 48

Rue would do a lot of things. In the past, I'd witnessed her ruthlessness firsthand. Witnessed her running roughshod over the rules, and sometimes other people, to get what she wanted. A prime example was how she blackmailed her way into viewing the security footage that placed Brodie in Harker on the night of the killing. But, for all Rue's faults, she wasn't a killer.

"Did you search Evan's trailer?" I asked Danny.

"Is that how I investigate a crime? Thank you. I had no idea."

"Danny," Brodie warned.

His brother blew out an annoyed breath. "For your information, we did conduct a search."

My heart beat sped up. "And?"

"And we found nothing tying him to the murder or my attempted murder."

My shoulders slumped. In a twisted way, finding some evidence linking Evan to the killing, even a small drop of blood on a pair of shoes, would've made me feel better. As it was, the case against him was circumstantial at best. Danny and the DA had to know as much.

Unless they had more than Danny was letting on.

Brodie must've come to a similar conclusion, for he took a menacing step toward his brother. Unfortunately, with one eye closed, he mis-stepped and almost fell over the edge of Danny's desk. He caught himself in time.

"Sit down before you break something," Danny relented, "and I'll tell you about our other evidence."

"From inside the trailer?" I asked.

He shook his head.

"So you didn't find any baking supplies?"

"No."

"But you did look?"

"Brodie, you're my brother, and I love you, but I swear to God, if she insults me again, I'm going to toss you both in a cell for the next six months." Danny's glare grew hotter with each word.

I winced. "I didn't mean to question your abilities. It's just . . ."

"The last time we were in Evan's trailer it was a mess. Full of

156

pizza boxes and beer cans. Nothing to indicate he could or would bake a batch of poisoned cookies. Is that what you're thinking, Charms?"

"Precisely."

Danny frowned. "I'd already considered as much. But he could've bought them, or baked them at someone else's house."

Or, far more likely, someone else tried to poison Danny, and frame me.

The thought burned into my head like whiskey at the back of the throat.

Danny rose from his chair, pacing in front of us. "I know what you're thinking, but we have the right person. Follow me, and I'll prove it." He motioned to the door. Slowly Brodie followed, me a step or two behind him. We headed down the hallway, back toward the interrogation room. Danny stopped, ushering us inside a small dark room that smelled faintly of chemicals, like a janitor's closet. Was he planning to lock us in until we agreed with him? I wouldn't put it past him.

He gestured to a large window and an intercom next to it. Brodie pressed his finger to the device. The sound of crying echoed from its depths. I peered through the window, as tears slid down my cousin's cheeks on the other side of the two-way mirror.

"He'll crack," Danny said with confidence and then turned on his heel, leaving Brodie and me alone, in the dimly lit closet, for lack of a better word. I gripped my hands together, half hoping Danny was right. For one thing, I wouldn't have to worry about being framed for additional murders.

"What do you think?" Brodie nodded to my cousin beyond the glass.

I shrugged.

"Me too."

In the silence that followed, we watched as Danny entered the interrogation room, winking at us before taking a seat across from Evan. Expecting Danny to play the role of bad cop, I was surprised when he offered Evan a soda and a candy bar from the vending machine. When Evan declined, Danny said, "Tell me about your relationship with Marcus Savage."

Evan, snot bubbling from his nose, told Danny the same thing he had me. I blushed as Brodie listened to the explanation. Not only was I embarrassed by my cousin's betrayal, but being the dupe in Marcus's plot multiplied my distress.

Brodie gripped the edge of the window as Evan went on. "That bastard."

I wholeheartedly agreed, but stayed quiet.

"He had to know you'd never sell." Brodie frowned. "Married or not."

"Marcus wasn't used to not getting his way. He probably thought that I'd go along with whatever he wanted, after, of course, he got you out of the way."

Brodie snorted. "He didn't know you very well."

I nodded. "No, he did not."

We shared a small laugh.

Our humor faded as Danny pressed Evan on his whereabouts at the time of Marcus's murder. Evan insisted he was at home, alone. Though not a single soul could support his alibi. "Wait," he said. "My car was parked outside my trailer. One of my neighbors had to see it."

Danny looked skeptical at best. A look his brother shared.

"This isn't getting us anywhere," Brodie said with disgust as Evan broke down in tears once again. His cell phone buzzed before he could say more. Glancing at the screen, he held up his finger. "Sorry, Charms. I really need to take this." He stepped out of the room, phone to his ear.

I looked through the glass once more, listening to Danny question my cousin until I thought Danny's head might explode. His face grew redder and redder as Evan cried his way through every question. A young deputy who I didn't recognize knocked on the door about ten minutes later. "Ms. Lucky," he said, "Mr. Gett had to leave, but he said he'd call you later."

Since Danny was still in with Evan, that left only one Mr. Gett. "Did Brodie say where he was going?"

"No, ma'am. But he did say you should go home."

I held in an eye roll. "Thank you," I said to the deputy. With a sigh, my attention returned to the seemingly endless, albeit very wet interrogation.

Chapter 49

As I left the sheriff's office, I couldn't stop replaying Evan's words in my head. Someone wanted to buy Lucky Whiskey badly enough to commit marriage, but what about murder? And who, if not Rue? Furthermore, how was I going to tell Jack about Evan's betrayal? Being suspected of murder was one thing to a man like Jack, but selling out family was quite another.

I climbed into the truck, cranking the engine. It sputtered to life, groaning much like its owner did when he rose from his favorite chair. I considered returning home like Brodie ordered. Lucky needed some work, especially after the still had blown. I would, once again, try and fix it, or patch it the best I could until I could find the money to replace it. I would find the money somehow.

Driving past the Harker Motel, my eyes drifted to the room where Marcus had expired. My foot hit the brake and my hands turned the wheel into the parking lot. I pulled to a stop outside Wendell's office. The shutters were closed and it appeared as if no one was inside. I blew out a sigh as I jumped down from the driver's seat and onto the heated pavement under my feet. The scent of tar mixed with exhaust fumes tickled my nostrils. I knocked on the door to the office, and when Wendell didn't answer, I climbed the stairs up to the room where Marcus had died less than a week before.

The railing under my fingertips felt cold, even in the heat of the day.

I hoped the room would be unlocked, and luck, as always, wasn't on my side. The door was shut tight, refusing to budge no matter how hard I twisted the knob. I looked to the room where Grace was staying. It too looked dark and empty. Had she checked out?

My eyes darted to the parking lot below. Two parking spaces sat directly between where Marcus had stayed and Grace's room. A blue Chevy sat in one of the spots, tilting to one side, as if riding on a flat tire. My eyes narrowed.

The vehicle had been parked in that very space on Saturday, when I'd come to Marcus's room to end our engagement, and then again on the day Brodie and I broke into the motel room. I remembered it clearly because I'd nearly opened the door of Grace's car into the side of it.

"Hey, Charlotte," Wendell called from below. He held up his hand, covering his eyes from the sun's glare. "Did you need a room?"

"No, but I do have a question for you."

"Shoot."

Climbing down the steps, I waved to the car. "Does one of your guests drive this car?"

"Why? You interested in buying it?"

"What? No."

His face fell. "Oh. I've been trying to sell this piece of junk for a month. It belonged to my mother-in-law, but since the wife and I took her keys, we've been kinda stuck with it."

"Sorry to hear it." I licked my lips as a thought occurred to me. "Has it been in that spot all along?"

He waved to the hood. "Yeah. It needs a new alternator, and I haven't gotten around to fixing it yet."

"Can I have the key to that room?" I pointed to the downed yellow crime scene tape flapping in the wind in front of Marcus's room.

He dug in his pocket for what I assumed was a master key. "I haven't had a chance to clean it yet, but you're welcome to it."

I took the key and raced up the steps. A few seconds later, I was standing at the window, staring at the lot below. Sure enough, only two spots were visible below. The first of which was the one with the Chevy parked in it. The other was empty.

But it hadn't been a few days ago.

Chapter 50

I dialed Brodie's cell number while keeping one hand on the steering wheel. The road back to Gett might've been paved with good intentions, but it was also full of ruts. I'd already nearly lost control after hitting a wide pothole. Of course, speed was a factor as I'd kept the gas pedal against the floor since leaving the Harker Motel.

His voice mail answered after the fourth ring. Damn. "I think Grace was lying about seeing Evan's car. Or maybe she was just mistaken. I don't see a reason for her to lie about it. Anyway, I'm on my way to ask her about it." I hesitated. "Call me."

The phone flew out of my hand, hitting the floorboard with a thud as the pickup lurched into another hole. Why hadn't I extended my AppleCare? With a sigh, I turned up the road toward Grace's house. A red BMW rushed past me at top speed, nearly running into me. I slammed on the brakes, skidding to a stop to avoid a collision. Was that Grace's car? And just where was she going in such a hurry? Fearing she'd had one too many again, I flipped around to follow her but her car had already vanished from view.

She couldn't have gone far, plus there wasn't really many places to go in Gett—the diner, either of the watering holes, or the church. Seeing as it wasn't Sunday, the church seemed unlikely. I decided to check the local watering holes first. Not only for Grace, but for Brodie as well.

Sadly, neither Brodie's Jeep nor Grace's BMW was in the parking lot of either bar. Which left the diner. I drove along Main Street, as always impressed by the bright emerald green of the lawns. It was as if the color only existed to make those of us with black thumbs jealous.

My cell phone buzzed. I pulled to a stop, stretching to reach it, my fingers brushing the edge. It buzzed for a third time. Unhooking my seat belt, I dove for it, catching it on the fourth ring. "Hello." My phone died, the screen going black, as the call vanished into the ether.

I tossed the busted phone on the seat. I didn't have six hundred dollars to replace it, let alone a thousand or so for the latest and coolest version. I had a new still to buy, and employees to pay. An iPhone came last on my list. For a moment, the enormity of my responsibilities threatened to overwhelm me. My head dropped to the steering wheel. I took a slow, easy breath. And then another.

As the anxiety faded, I started the engine once more, pulling back into traffic. Which, in Gett, was three or four cars in a mile stretch. The diner came into view on the left, the parking lot nearly empty. Cindy Mae's car, a late-model minivan with multiple kids' car seats inside, was the only one in the lot. I grinned at how different the life of the former Gett prom queen had turned out.

Like Cindy Mae, I hadn't quite expected how changed my life would be after Jack's heart attack. I surely hadn't expected to be running all over Gett trying to solve the murder of a man who claimed to love me for financial gain.

I drove up Main Street, hoping for a glimpse of Grace's BMW. Luck, for once, was on my side as I spotted it in the parking lot of the church.

Along with a black Jeep.

Brodie's black Jeep to be precise. Had he heard my voice mail and went searching for Grace? I released the breath I hadn't known I'd been holding and pulled into the spot next to his Jeep.

Other than our vehicles the lot was empty. A piece of crumbled paper drifted past me as I headed for the wooden doors of the church. The loud retort of a gunshot sounded.

I jerked back. My heart slammed wildly as I searched my body for telltale signs of blood and guts. Finding none, I started for the church doors. In hindsight, running toward the sound of a gunshot wasn't the brightest of moves. In my defense, I wasn't thinking clearly. My only thoughts were of Brodie.

However, I wasn't completely foolish. I slipped quietly into the church, staying to the side, in case any bullets flew my way. Rather than gunshots, the only sounds were of a muffled argument. I recognized Pastor Matt's calming voice.

I poked my head around the corner. In front of the altar he stood, his hands outstretched. Grace stood with her back to me, a gun in her hand. The barrel swung in the pastor's direction. She waved it back and forth from him to the floor.

I took a tentative step up the aisle, crouching in hopes she wouldn't see me. My plan, formed in a moment of hazy terror, was to get close enough to grab the gun. Another step in brought me closer, giving me a view of what she was pointing to on the floor.

Unbidden, a scream burst from my lips before I could stop it.

Chapter 51

I ran forward, to the man lying facedown on the floor. I knelt, pressing my hand against Brodie's throat, praying for a pulse. Thankfully it beat steady and strong under my fingertips, surprising since the carpet beneath him was soaked with blood. If I didn't do something soon he would die.

I looked up, straight into the barrel of Grace's gun. She would kill me, Pastor Matt and Brodie without a second thought. The intent was clear in the darkening of her eyes. "Why? Why are you doing this?" I asked in a strangled voice. Though I had a pretty good idea it was related to Marcus's murder. I just didn't quite see how.

"Don't act like you don't know," she hissed.

I only wished I was that good of an actress. Brodie's groan captured my attention. "Please. Call for help."

She laughed at my request.

My eyes shifted to the pastor, who stood grim-faced in front of her. With my gaze, I pleaded with him to do something. Anything really. And he did, just not what I'd expected.

"Shoot her and let's be done with it," he said. "I'm so sick of this town. The sooner we're out of here the better."

Shock froze me in place. Not only at his words, but at the casual way he spoke of my outright murder.

"But we still need the password to Savage's phone," she whined in an unbecoming tone.

He shrugged. "It doesn't matter anymore. The money cleared our account this morning. We can give up the game and disappear for good now."

The game? What game? The question left my mind when Grace nodded, steadying the gun aimed at my head.

"I can give you Marcus's password," I lied, stalling for time.

Matt, as I refused to think of him as Pastor Matt anymore, laughed. "You had your chance. Just like Savage. He should've taken what we offered and none of this would be happening."

"I'm nothing like Marcus," I said, a smile spreading across my face. "All this time I knew it was you who killed him, but did I say a word?" I shook my head. "I am playing my own game."

Matt raised an eyebrow. "I knew your innocent act was just

that, an act. No one teams up with their enemy like that." He looked to Grace, and then back at me. "So what's the con? Are you trying to get Gett there" — he nudged Brodie with his foot — "to marry you?"

"Yes." I clung to the lifeline Matt had offered. Hoping it would keep Brodie and me alive.

Grace snorted. "You're lying. Badly too. A pro doesn't fall for their mark."

She was half right in her estimation.

Matt took the gun from Grace's hand. "Is that right, Charlotte? Are you in love with Gett there?" He jerked the weapon in Brodie's direction. "What do you say I shoot him, and we'll find out if she's telling the truth or not."

"No," I yelled, using my body to cover Brodie's, or as much of it as I could.

Before he could pull the trigger, the whoop of a police siren ripped through the air. Matt swung toward the church doors. The next thing I knew, Brodie's hand shot out, capturing Matt's right leg. He jerked him down hard. The gun flew up the aisle.

"Run, Charms!" Brodie yelled, his voice laced with pain.

I did as he said, right toward the fallen weapon. Grace had a similar idea, as she sprinted toward the gun, hands outstretched. She had a few steps on me so I did the only thing I could think of, I tackled her, both of us flying into the pews. We landed hard, Grace on top of me. The air had left my lungs in a whoosh, leaving me momentarily stunned. Grace took advantage of my stunned state, wrapping her hands around my throat. The diamond of her large-carat wedding ring cut into my skin.

Over the last nine months, working daily in the distillery, I'd developed muscles I hadn't known existed. Muscles now engaged in a battle for my very life. I used my knee to lift Grace off me. I followed up with a fist to the side of her head. Pain rocketed through my hand, and my fingers went numb. She dropped to the ground, unconscious.

I leapt up in time to see Matt wrap his fingers around the handle of the gun.

The deafening roar of gunfire rocked the church.

Brodie crumpled to the ground.

Chapter 52

A few hours later, I sat on a hard plastic chair, exhaustion weighing heavily. My shoulders hung down, as if unable to bear much more. Danny Gett paced in front of me, his face hard and cold. He looked as if he'd aged ten years in a matter of hours. Honestly, I was so damn happy to see him, I didn't care that he stopped to glare at me every few minutes.

A man in a white doctor's coat pushed through the emergency room doors, looking around until his eyes fell on Danny. I held my breath as he came forward. "I'm sorry, Sheriff Gett, but the damage was too great. We lost him."

Stone-faced, Danny did nothing more than nod.

Bile rose up my throat but I swallowed it down. Tears burned my eyes for what could have been.

"Are you seriously tearing up for the guy, Charms?" Brodie said from the chair next to me. "He nearly killed us. Remember?"

I nodded stiffy. "My tears aren't for Pastor Matt . . . or whatever his name was." Who wasn't really a pastor, or named Matt apparently. Pastor Matt had turned out to be, according to his fingerprints, a con man wanted up and down the coast for crimes ranging from fraud to outright murder, along with his accomplice, a woman known only as the Widow. Together, the pair had married and poisoned over seven wealthy men.

"Then why are you crying?" he asked, taking my hand in his warm, good one. A sling was wrapped around his other arm, where Grace had shot him before I'd arrived at the church. Luckily the bullet hadn't lodged anywhere vital, though he'd lost plenty of blood.

"If Danny hadn't burst into the church, and shot Matt, he would've killed us." I shivered at the memory of the coldness in his face moments before his death at Danny's hands.

Brodie squeezed my fingers. I winced in pain, my hand still aching from when I punched Grace. Though I'd do it again in a heartbeat. And not only because it stopped her from reaching the gun. "I thought we decided that the next time I gave you an order, you'd do what I asked," he said.

"You know better than that. I will never take orders from a Gett."

He snorted. Danny turned to glare at us once again. I gave him a broad smile. Somehow he'd rushed in at the right moment, saving our lives. "How did you know where to find us?" I asked him.

One of his dark eyebrows rose in question.

I flushed. The question had held an edge of unintended accusation. "I meant, what made you suspect Matt and Grace of Marcus's murder?"

For a long moment I thought he wouldn't answer. Finally he admitted, "I didn't. Not until I walked in on that damn pastor about to pull the trigger."

"I don't understand." I shook my head. "Why else would you come to the church?"

Brodie answered instead. "I called him."

Danny nodded.

"When I stepped out to take that phone call," Brodie said, "I overheard the cops say the substance found in your kitchen and the cookies baked for Danny was *Cerbera odollam*. A type of poison found only in southern Asia. Places like Afghanistan."

"Or India," I said.

"Bingo," Brodie said with a grin. "The good pastor had bragged about his trip to India, and it got me to thinking. I called Danny right before I decided to have a quick look around the church. I never saw Grace. Or the gun. Not until it was too late."

"Going there alone wasn't the smartest thing to do," I said.

He shrugged, and then winced. "About as bright as running into gunfire."

"I saved your life."

He snorted. "I had them right where I . . . Hell with it. Yes. Yes, you did. But my plan wasn't to get caught searching the church. The ladies' auxiliary said the good pastor would be with them, preparing for the bake sale all afternoon, so I took a chance."

"And nearly died."

A dark eyebrow rose. "Are you going to keep bringing that up?"

"Yes." I blew out a tense breath. "Did you find any poison before Grace caught you?"

He nodded. "In plain sight. A big green plant sitting in the pastor's office. They didn't even try to hide it."

"Probably because no one else would know how deadly it was," Danny grumbled.

"True."

Danny suddenly spoke up. "The ME is going to rerun the toxicology report on Jonas, but chances are they poisoned him."

I ran my hand over my face. "But why kill Marcus? Was he somehow involved with them? And what about the paparazzo? Why did they try to kill him?"

My questions remained unanswered until a few days later.

Chapter 53

Brodie drove over to Lucky, with one arm still in his sling, days later. He handed me Marcus's iPhone, and then sat on the wicker chair on my porch. I frowned. "What am I supposed to do with this?"

"You said you had the password," he said with a quick grin. "Of course, you also said you planned on marrying me."

"You wish," I said, my face heating. Since that afternoon in the church, Matt's words had haunted me. How did I really feel about Brodie? I knew we had something more than a friendship, but how much more?

"Relax, Charms. Danny had his guys crack the phone, so you are off the hook," he said with a laugh.

"What is on it?"

He waved to it. "Why don't you find out for yourself?"

I did just that. I swiped my finger across the screen. A picture of Marcus, handsome and smiling, popped up on the wallpaper. With a shallow breath, I pressed a few apps without anything sinister appearing.

And then I touched the photos app, and a rush of photos, all taken in the days before he died, appeared on the screen.

One in particular caught my eye.

A shot of Marcus on the balcony of the Harker Motel. His face intent on the camera. A picture that would've sent a rush of jubilation along the nerves of his fans.

It did just that for me. But for a far different reason.

Marcus had taken more than just a selfie. Through a crack in the curtain of the motel room next door, Grace was locked in a passionate embrace with the good pastor.

The photo was dated the night of Jack's party.

"Looks pretty bad for a widow to be kissing the pastor on the night her husband dies." Brodie motioned to the iPhone.

I grinned. "The champagne in the background isn't a good look either."

"Very true." We shared a small laugh. "Danny says Grace admitted to killing Marcus. Of course, she said it was all Pastor Matt's idea. And who is he to argue." Brodie shook his head.

"Once you refused to marry him, Savage tried his hand at blackmail. I doubt he realized the extent of their extended body count, and wound up dead for his troubles."

"That's why Matt kept asking questions about Marcus." I nodded as if it made complete sense. "They were trying to get his password so they could delete the picture. Why didn't they just leave town?"

"Money." Brodie shook his head. "Jonas hid a lot of it right before his death. Money embezzled from the Savings & Loan. Which is why the Savings & Loan couldn't give you the loan you need for the still. Not some Gett plot to destroy Lucky." He twirled an invisible mustache like a villain. "That comes later."

My head snapped up, eyes narrowing. "How did you know . . . ?"

". . . That you thought I'd ruined your chance at getting the loan? I can read you like a book, luv."

I tried to stop my heart from leaping at the endearment. Rather than let him see how rattled it made me, I snarked, "Gee, I didn't know Getts can read."

He laughed.

"What about the cameraman? Why did they attack him? Was he helping Marcus blackmail them?"

Brodie shook his head slowly. "Andy, the camera guy, woke up late yesterday and told Danny all about his attack." A smile flickered over his lips. Not the sort of reaction I expected when talking about attempted murder. "The night he got to town, seems Andy met a lovely woman at the Gett Bar, a woman he spent the next evening getting to know a whole lot better."

"Grace?"

"Betty Marshall."

"Oh." I winced. Betty Marshall was well-known around Gett. So was her very jealous and ham-fisted husband, Winston.

"Danny arrested Winston for assault this morning."

"So that's it?"

"Not quite," Brodie said, his eyes heating as he leaned forward. Closer and closer.

I met him halfway, ready to take a chance on whatever it was between us.

"There he is," Jack, leaning on his cane, walked onto the porch, a wide smile on his face, which slipped when he caught sight of us. I jumped back, upending the glass of sweet tea I'd placed next to Brodie when he'd arrived. It tipped forward, spilling, ice cubes and all, on to his lap.

He leapt up with a curse. One of the four-letter variety.

"I expect you to refrain from such talk in front of Charlotte in the future, boy," Jack admonished. "She's a lady."

I held back a snort, which abruptly turned into a chuckle when one of Brodie's eyebrows lifted.

"I'll keep that in mind," Brodie said.

"See that you do." Jack's face split into a wide grin. "We can't have a partner talking like that. Harms morale."

A sick feeling rose in my stomach. "Partner?"

Jack looked sheepishly from Brodie to me. "Well, Char . . . you see . . ."

Brodie frowned. "You didn't tell her?"

"No, son," Jack admitted. "Would you?"

"I see your point," Brodie said when he looked over at me.

"Tell me what?" I strangled out. My vision grew red as seconds ticked by without an answer.

Chapter 54

"What did you do?!?" I asked Jack in a near shout. "He's a Gett."

"Take it easy, Charms," Brodie said. "You need an infusion of cash, and I have cash to infuse. Simple as that."

Never trust a Gett bearing gifts was the Lucky family motto. I'd be foolish to ignore that advice now. So why was Jack? And how much cash were we talking about? The possibility of a shiny new still leapt to my mind, followed by the very real probability that working with Brodie would drive me insane. "How . . . how did this happen?"

"The boy came to me a few days ago. He made an offer"—a smile spilt Jack's weathered face—"that I couldn't refuse. An offer that would pay for that new still you had your eyes on."

Brodie offered Jack over two hundred thousand dollars? A question came to mind. First, where had Brodie gotten that kind of money? From his grandmother most likely. But that couldn't be. Jack would never take money from Rue, even if in a roundabout way. I risked asking as much. "Since you haven't worked in over a year, just where did you get that sort of money?"

Jack's face reddened, but Brodie seemed unaffected by my question. He smiled instead, which set my teeth on edge. "Maybe I sold an engagement ring or two."

"You are hilarious," I said, deadpan.

He laughed. "When I was overseas, I decided to invest in some real estate."

I raised an eyebrow. Brodie, in his worn Levi's, looked like a blue-collar worker rather than a real estate mogul. "What sort of real estate?"

"For your information, I am the proud owner of the Gett Bar & Grill." He grinned at my snort. "Willow, I'll admit, does most of the work, but I do pitch in from time to time." A slight pause filled the air. "Which is how I see our new partnership."

I couldn't stop the bitter laugh bubbling from my lips. This was all too much. Surely Jack was playing a prank. Any time now he'd say, *Gotcha*. When Jack didn't, I glared at Brodie. "I'd rather drink a cask of Gett."

"That only proves you have good taste." Brodie smiled, all gleaming white teeth. "Now, we should update our distribution channels . . ."

About the Author

When she isn't looking for a place to hide the bodies, J. A. (Julie) Kazimer spends her time with a pup named Killer. Other hobbies include murdering houseplants and avoiding housework. She spent a few years as a bartender and then wasted another few years stalking people while working as a private investigator before transitioning to become a writer and penning over fifteen titles. She lives in Denver. Visit her website at jakazimer.com.